ROCK HARBOR
LOST
&FOUND

ROCK HARBOR
LOST & FOUND

by Colleen Coble
and Robin Caroll

THOMAS NELSON
Since 1798

NASHVILLE   DALLAS   MEXICO CITY   RIO DE JANEIRO

Published in Nashville, Tennessee, by Tommy Nelson. Tommy Nelson is a registered trademark of Thomas Nelson, Inc.

Tommy Nelson titles may be purchased in bulk for educational, business, fund-raising, or sales promotional use. For information, please e-mail SpecialMarkets@ThomasNelson.com.

Unless otherwise noted, Scripture quotations are taken from the Holy Bible, New International Version®, NIV®. © 1973, 1978, 1984, 2011 by Biblica, Inc.™ Used by permission of Zondervan. All rights reserved worldwide. www.zondervan.com

Library of Congress Cataloging-in-Publication Data

Coble, Colleen.
    Rock Harbor lost and found / by Colleen Coble ; with Robin Caroll.
        pages cm—(Rock Harbor Search and Rescue series)
    Summary: When fourteen-year-old Emily O'Reilly learns that her best friend, Olivia Webster, was adopted, the two seek Olivia's birth parents, but meanwhile, Emily's mother Marika is released on parole and will stop at nothing to contact her daughter.
    ISBN 978-1-4003-2163-6 (pbk.)
    [1. Adoption—Fiction. 2. Mothers and daughters—Fiction. 3. Missing persons-
-Fiction. 4. Search dogs—Fiction. 5. Rescue dogs—Fiction. 6. Dogs—Fiction. 7. Christian life—Fiction. 8. Mystery and detective stories.] I. Coble, Colleen. II. Title.
PZ7.C6355Rnl 2013
[Fic]—dc23   2013014704

Printed in the United States of America

13 14 15 16 17 RRD 6 5 4 3 2 1

For Alexa Coble,
who brightens her Mimi's life every day

 **ONE**

Something wasn't quite right.

Wrinkling her nose, Emily O'Reilly took a step back and stared at the centerpiece she'd just finished putting together. The big blue-and-gray crepe paper *C* looked lopsided somehow.

"What did you do to that?" Olivia Webster, Emily's best friend, asked with a giggle.

"I followed the instructions . . . at least most of them." At fourteen, Emily thought she could manage a centerpiece without directions, but maybe she should have read them after all.

Olivia giggled again and reached for Emily's pathetic attempt at decorating. "You're hopeless, Em." Within seconds, she had the centerpiece level and looking like the others sitting on tables across the Rock Harbor Community Center. Olivia was a genius when it came to that sort of thing.

Emily? Not so much.

"Why are we decorating so early anyway? The celebration isn't until the weekend." Emily shoved the decoration's wrapping into the bag of trash she'd carried from table to table. "It's only Monday."

"Because we want everything to be perfect." Olivia pushed in a chair, straightened the glitter-littered tablecloth, and lifted the bag of trash. "It's too much to do all at once, and we don't want anything to get forgotten."

Emily sighed and followed her best friend. How, again, had she let Olivia talk her into serving on the homecoming celebration committee?

"It's going to be beautiful." Olivia tossed the bag into the trash can. "I can't wait."

Emily had to admit that everything did look really nice. And the night of the celebration would be epic—lots of food, lots of music, and lots of dancing. Dad and Naomi, Emily's stepmom, would probably slow dance. *That* would be embarrassing.

"Come on, let's head to my house. Mom and Dad should still be at the movies." Olivia led the way out of the front door.

The community center was one of the most beautiful buildings in town, built by Rock Harbor's early residents during the Copper Queen mining hype. Emily loved the building's really cool high ceilings and fun corners to explore.

Emily followed as the other volunteers spilled out onto Houghton Street. "I hope they don't get home sooner than you think." She jumped onto her bicycle and pedaled after her best friend.

A late-fall breeze tugged at Emily's hair, pushing a hint of the distinct scent of Lake Superior across the parking lot.

"Me too. But the movie isn't supposed to be over for"—Olivia checked her watch, her bike wobbling—"another forty minutes. It'll take them at least thirty to drive back home." She bumped over the curb and onto the sidewalk.

They biked down Houghton Street and passed the familiar

sights of town. Rock Harbor might be smaller than some towns in Michigan's Upper Peninsula, but it more than made up for it with the quaintness of the town with its Victorian buildings and community activities. Soon the residents would own the town alone again. The summer and early fall tourist season was almost over now that winter was on its way in.

The girls coasted up Olivia's driveway and propped their bikes against the carport. Olivia unlocked the side door with the key she wore on a chain around her neck, hidden safely under her shirt.

Emily shut the door behind them. "I'm so glad Naomi thought of using your parents' wedding picture as the design for the anniversary cake. The baker said she needed a copy right away though. Do you have any idea where to look?"

"They used to have it out when I was a little girl. I'm not sure where Mom put it when we moved to this house." Olivia pulled out the top drawer in the desk by the door to the hall.

Emily moved to the bookcase and looked. "Did you know the first marriage license was issued in the mid-eighteen hundreds?"

"No, I didn't, and I don't understand why you even know that." Olivia shook her head, grinning, then turned back to the drawer. "You and your random facts."

Emily loved history—the more random, the better. Maybe that's why she loved being on the History Smackdown team so much.

"Do they have an office?" Emily asked. She should know because she'd spent the night there lots of times, but they usually hung out in Olivia's room. She'd been in the living room, the kitchen, and Olivia's room, but nowhere else.

"No. We have this computer desk, but that's about it." Olivia opened the next drawer. "But I'm not seeing any pictures."

"What about an attic?"

Olivia grinned. "The way you love attics is a little weird. But we only have a nasty one that you get to with a pull-down ladder, and it's full of insulation. Dad doesn't store anything up there. Mom says it's a death trap."

"Then where do they store stuff like your Christmas tree?"

"Oh! There's some attic space over the garage. We'll check if nothing's in the drawers."

Emily glanced through the books in the bookcase but found no photo albums. "Nothing here."

"Nothing here either." Olivia slammed the last desk drawer. "Let's check the garage."

Emily followed her to the garage, and together they managed to get the ladder pulled down. The exertion left Emily huffing. "How much time do we have left?"

Olivia disappeared up the ladder. "About a half hour." Her voice was muffled.

"We'd better hurry then. We'll need to get out of here so they don't know we came by." The girls were supposed to go to Emily's after helping out at the community center, but Naomi knew they were coming by to get the picture.

Olivia's face appeared in the hole above her. "There's nothing here but the Christmas tree and some boxes of ornaments."

"They have to keep things like this somewhere."

Olivia came back down the ladder, and the girls shoved it back into place. Olivia had a smudge of dirt on her cheek, and Emily brushed it off.

"Now what?" Emily asked.

"I didn't want to go into Mom and Dad's room. They keep it shut. But I think we have to. We don't have any other option, I guess."

Emily raised her brows. "You never go in there? Not even to crawl in bed with your mom and watch a movie or something?"

Olivia shook her head. "They don't have a TV in their bedroom."

"Haven't you even taken your parents breakfast in bed or something?"

Olivia just shook her head and led the way back inside the house.

Emily scrunched up her nose. There was something fishy about that. Emily and her two brothers loved piling on the bed whenever Dad didn't have to work. And sometimes even just with Naomi. Emily and Timmy always made Dad and Naomi breakfast in bed on their birthdays and for Mother's Day and Father's Day. But, Olivia was an only child. Maybe that changed things. Olivia's parents were crazy about Olivia though. And every family was different.

Standing outside the closed door to the bedroom, Emily's pulse sped up. "What if your mom catches us in here? Will we get in trouble?"

Olivia turned the doorknob. "No, she'll just tell me bedrooms are meant to be private places and should only be entered by invitation."

"Weird," Emily muttered. If she disobeyed a standing house rule, Dad would ground her. At least take away her phone for a week.

Olivia shoved the door open. "She says it's because she wants to teach me about boundaries."

"That makes sense I guess." Emily peered past the doorway

into the bedroom. It was way neater than Dad and Naomi's. The bed didn't have a wrinkle, and the tables and dressers were cleared and held only a vase with fake flowers and a statuette. "No pictures here."

"There's one place I want to check. Mom's trunk." Olivia pointed to the foot of the bed where a cedar chest stood. There was a lacy coverlet draped over the shiny wood.

Emily could see Olivia's hesitation, so she stepped past her and lifted the cover to reveal the top. The lid rose easily, and the aroma of cedar wafted to her nose. She inhaled. "I love that smell."

Olivia knelt beside her. "Me too. And I think we've found the right place. There are all kinds of pictures and documents in here. Look, here's their marriage license."

It was nicely framed in black. "We can use it if we can't find their wedding photo." Emily laid it aside. "Here it is!" She pulled out the wedding photo showing a younger version of Olivia's parents posing together. "Your mom is so pretty." With Mrs. Webster's bright blue eyes and natural blond hair, she could've been a model.

"Yes, she is. I always wished I looked like her. I don't know who I look like though."

There was a picture under the wedding photo of a baby with a man and a woman. The woman was holding the little girl and smiling down at her. Emily picked it up. "Aw, too cute. How old were you here?"

She turned over the photo and froze when she read the words on the back: *At Tarver's office the day of Olivia's adoption. July 13. She was three months old. Happy day!*

Adopted? Liv was adopted? Emily's gaze flashed to Olivia, but words wouldn't come.

Olivia reached for the photo. "What's it say?"

Too late, Emily tried to pull it away, but Olivia's fingers held it in place while she read it. Emily was almost afraid to see her friend's expression, but she couldn't look away.

Olivia's eyes widened, and the color drained from her cheeks. "A-adopted?" Her voice was thick, then her fingers went slack, and the picture fell from her hand.

Emily touched her shoulder. "Liv? You okay?"

"I—I knew there was something . . ." Her words choked off. "I thought I was just imagining things, you know? I don't look like either one of them."

Emily wished she knew what to say. She could only imagine how she would feel to find out she was adopted. Marika was a horrible mother, but at least Emily knew who she was. "What are you going to do?"

The tears were rolling down Olivia's face now. "I don't know. I can't admit to them that I found it without telling them I was in the chest. And they'll want to know why I was in there. I don't want to spoil the surprise."

Just like Olivia to think of everyone else's feelings before her own. "Maybe you can start asking questions about seeing baby pictures and stuff. I bet they've wanted to tell you but weren't sure how," Emily suggested.

"Maybe." Olivia got up and put the picture away. "We have to get out of here before Mom comes back. Just pray for me, Em." She straightened the coverlet back over the top of the cedar chest.

Her voice was choked. "You know I will, Liv. I'm sorry."

"Me too, Em. Me too. But you know what this means, don't you?"

Emily nodded. "You need to know who your real parents are. And I'll help you."

Olivia . . . adopted.

Emily couldn't wrap her mind around it, and she ached for her friend. She didn't even know how she'd feel if she found out she was adopted. She stared up at the picture in the *Phantom of the Opera* frame sitting on the shelf over her computer. Taken last year, it was Naomi and Dad and Timmy and Matthew and her with Charley at their feet. The whole family hugged one another and smiled for the camera.

Sherlock growled.

Emily giggled at her puppy as he growled again, then pounced on the chew toy that had fallen off the edge of his bed by her desk. She hadn't even had him a month, and already she loved her puppy so much. She couldn't imagine giving him up now . . . it would break her heart.

Who were Olivia's real parents, and why had they given her up? Why hadn't Mr. and Mrs. Webster told Olivia she was adopted? Lots of kids were adopted, so it wasn't like it was something to keep secret.

The back of the picture had said, *At Tarver's office*. Who was Tarver? Maybe the person at the adoption agency?

Emily quickly opened the browser on her computer, then ran a search for adoption agencies in the Upper Peninsula. Over forty-five results loaded. Forty-five? Sheesh, they'd never get through that many. She then ran a search for "adoptions in the Upper Peninsula" and "Tarver." Only two results loaded: Les Tarver and Charlotte Tarver, both listed as attorneys specializing in private adoptions. Les Tarver had an office in Ishpeming, which was about an hour and a half to two hours away, while

Charlotte's office was in Marquette, one of the closest towns to Rock Harbor. Emily jotted down the information.

She opened two new tabs and began searches on both Les and Charlotte Tarver. She waited for both pages to load. The results on Les Tarver returned first. Emily read a few of the posts only to find Les Tarver had retired from the legal profession four years ago. If he was the attorney who handled Olivia's adoption, finding information might be difficult.

There were many more results on Charlotte Tarver. Pictures of her winning various legal awards, news articles about her work, and her website. Emily clicked on the website. She scanned the information, then found the Contact Us form. Should she fill it out? Olivia might not want her to. She hesitated for a moment, then typed a message stating she had some questions regarding adoptions approximately fourteen years ago.

"Timmy! Emily! Matthew! Dinner," Naomi called.

Emily clicked Send on the message, then closed the browser windows. It'd be nice if she got a response tomorrow. Maybe she and Olivia could ask Inetta Harris to help them with the research. She'd done so before, helping Emily clear her name when she'd been accused of stealing a valuable necklace. Yeah, she'd ask Inetta for help.

The phone rang, and she answered it before looking at the caller ID. "Liv, you won't believe this." Too late she realized it was the house phone, not her cell phone. It wouldn't be Olivia. "Uh, sorry. This is the O'Reilly residence."

"Just who I wanted to talk to."

Emily froze at the familiar throaty voice. It was Marika. "You're not supposed to call here," Emily stammered. Her pulse raced, and she knew she should hang up, but wasn't that rude?

Six years ago, her mother Marika had been accused of attempted murder. She'd testified against her partner and had gotten a lighter sentence, and just last month had been released from prison. Emily could still remember all the horrors that had happened to her and Timmy because of their mother. No, in Emily's heart, Naomi was her real mother.

"I miss you, honey. You and Timmy. I've changed. Let me prove it to you."

She went hot then cold at the thought. "I have to go." She clicked off the phone, then hugged herself and held her breath when it rang again. Let Dad or Naomi get it this time. It stopped after three rings. She sat in front of the computer and fought tears. Not now. Marika couldn't be back in her life now.

Rapid footsteps sounded in the hall, then her father's familiar hard rap came on her door. "Emily."

She leaped up and threw open the door. One look in her dad's face, and she knew he'd talked to Marika.

"The next time she calls, just hang up. She's not allowed to have contact with you."

Relief flooded her. "Yes, sir. She caught me off guard."

His eyes softened, and he put his hand on his shoulder. "I know. It's time for supper."

He gave her a big hug, and then they joined the rest of the family at the table. Dad offered up the prayer, then everyone began to fill their plates. Despite the yummy smell of one of Emily's favorite meals, beef pasties, she really didn't feel like eating.

"And me and Dave, we're making a volcano for our science project. It's gonna really blow up and everything." Her little brother Timmy rattled on and on about school stuff. Usually his nonstop talking drove Emily crazy, but right now, his constant jabbering was a welcome distraction. It gave her time alone with her thoughts.

"What's with all the breads and cakes in the pantry?" Dad asked Naomi.

"Ladies' group at church. I'm delivering a basket to the waitresses over at the Copper Club later tonight." Naomi finished cutting up Matthew's food and pushed his plate back in front of him.

"Alone?"

"No. Bree is picking me up at nine."

Emily pushed her food around on her plate. She was really worried about Marika calling again, and she couldn't help but wonder how Olivia was. She'd sworn she wasn't going to tell her parents she'd found out, but Emily didn't know how. As it was, she wanted to tell Dad and Naomi about it but knew she couldn't. It wasn't her secret to tell, and Olivia had been betrayed enough.

"Emily, honey, is something wrong?"

She stared at Naomi from across the table. "Just not really hungry, I guess."

Dad cleared his throat. "Are you worried about Marika? I told her I'd press charges if she called again."

Emily nodded, but she was still worried. Marika never listened to anyone.

"You know we won't let anything happen to either of you." Dad included Timmy in his look.

"I know." Yet Emily just knew her mother would not give up easily.

And the thought of actually seeing Marika after everything she'd done terrified Emily right down to her bones.

TWO

"Did you talk to your parents?" Emily snatched a strand of hair that had escaped her ponytail and tucked it behind her ear. "I started to call you a million times but didn't want to interrupt."

The school's hallway was crowded with all the junior high kids. Emily had to move closer to Olivia to hear her since they didn't want to be overheard.

Olivia's brown eyes filled with tears. "I just couldn't say anything to them, Em. I mean, there has to be a reason they didn't tell me, right?"

Emily hugged her best friend. Tight. "I'm sorry, Liv. Really." She just couldn't imagine knowing such a big secret and *not* saying something.

Olivia shut her locker and leaned against it. "I started to bring it up more than a dozen times, then stopped myself." She pushed off the lockers and started down the hall.

Emily fell into step beside her. "Why?"

"They have to have a reason for not telling me. Something that would upset me if I found out."

"More than just knowing you're adopted?"

Olivia stopped and stared at her.

"I'm sorry. I just can't imagine not asking them."

"That's because your dad and Naomi are different from my parents. Mine are more . . . I don't know . . . formal about parenting." Olivia shrugged. "But maybe they act that way because I'm adopted."

"Don't be silly, Liv." Emily shifted her books and began heading to homeroom again. She had to turn sideways every now and again as someone brushed alongside her.

"Is it silly, Em? I mean, I'm wondering about everything they've ever said or done that I can remember. Every time someone said, 'Oh, you look just like your mother' or 'You have your father's smile,' they were wrong. It feels like my whole life is a big, fat lie."

Emily didn't know what to say, so she remained quiet and just continued walking. While it might not be a bad thing to find out Marika wasn't her mother, she couldn't imagine finding out her dad wasn't her dad.

"And who else knows? I mean, my parents couldn't have just had me appear with no explanation. Others have to know. People who never said a word to me." Olivia shook her head as she stepped around a group of kids huddled near their lockers. "I can't stop thinking about questions. Last night, I even had some crazy dreams."

"Like what?"

"Like about my birth parents."

Emily stopped outside of their homeroom class—English. The bell would ring soon, but she wanted to hear this. "What about them?"

"I couldn't see their faces, but they were arguing. My birth father hit her. She grabbed an infant—I'm guessing that was me—and told him she'd give the baby away before she let him hurt it." Olivia's eyes were wider than wide.

"Oh, wow." Emily's heartbeat kicked up a notch. She would've run straight to her parents' room if she'd had such a dream. "But that was just a dream, Liv. You were three months old when your parents adopted you, so there's no way you could remember something like that."

Olivia nodded. "I know, but I can't stop the questions running through my mind or my imagination from running away with me."

"You'll never get answers if you don't ask your parents."

"I know." Olivia stared at the floor. "I just can't bring myself to come right out and ask. I don't know. I think there's a real reason why they've never told me. Maybe it's something that makes them really sad, and if I bring it up, they'll get upset."

The bell rang, spurring on the kids to move faster through the halls. Several of their classmates' backpacks bumped against Emily and Olivia.

Emily pulled Olivia against the lockers, out of the main walkway. "Like what?"

"I don't know. I can't stop wondering if my birth parents are alive. If they are, and I ask my parents, will they feel like I'd rather be with them? Isn't that what happens on television?"

"C'mon, your parents know you love them."

"But if my birth parents are alive, why did they give me up for adoption?"

"Maybe they did it for your safety." Emily's thoughts raced with ideas. Dad always told her she watched too many true-crime television shows. "What if your birth father was killed by some really bad people and your birth mom had to go into witness protection? She *had* to give you up for adoption to be sure you'd be safe."

Olivia gave a weak smile. "Leave it to you to make this into a Hallmark movie."

"I'm sorry. That's just how my mind works. I'm really not trying to make a joke out of all this."

"And I can't say anything to them yet anyway . . . they'd ask why I was snooping around in Mom's trunk, and that would spoil the surprise of their anniversary party."

Emily sighed. They were really in a tight spot. *God, please help Olivia. She's got to have so many crazy emotions right now and just needs to feel loved. Please remind her that you love her more than any parent on earth.* Emily gave her best friend a smile and quickly told Olivia what she'd found out from her Internet searches last night.

"But what if those attorneys had nothing to do with my adoption? What if this Tarver person is actually a representative at one of those forty-five adoption agencies?"

"Then we'll go through all of them once we rule out the attorneys." Emily could hear the discouragement in Olivia's voice. She grabbed Olivia's arm and gave it a gentle squeeze. "We'll find out about your adoption, Liv. Even if we have to go through every single adoption agency in the state of Michigan."

"I guess."

"Maybe when I get home this afternoon there will be a reply from my e-mail to the Charlotte Tarver attorney. It could be the start."

Olivia flashed a feeble smile. "Thanks, Em. At least you're trying to figure things out without having to ask my parents."

"Hey, that's what best friends are for, right?"

"Right." Olivia moved to the English room door. "I have Fashion Club after school today, but that should only take an hour or so. Want to come over later and start researching?"

"I can't. Sherlock and I have training this afternoon. There's a competition coming up." Honestly, Emily was glad she didn't have to go over to the Websters'. While Olivia might be able to keep a secret, no way could Emily keep silent. Her mouth would open and the truth would jump out.

"Oh! I almost forgot to tell you, but Marika called last night," Emily blurted out.

Olivia's eyes went wide. "Wow, and here I am blubbering about being adopted. I'm sorry, Em. I know how much she scares you. What did she say?"

Emily told her. "But Dad says to hang up next time. I don't have to forgive her, do I, Liv?"

Olivia bit her lip. "You know you do, Emily."

"But I don't want to see her, much less forgive her!" Those were the last words she could get out before they had to enter class.

It was a little warmer in the training box out of the October wind. Emily sat scrunched in the small space and waited for Sherlock to find her. She could make out a muffled siren way off in the distance. The training day should have been tiring, but seeing how well her puppy was learning to search had energized her. Before long, he'd have Samson's search abilities.

Small paws scratched at the opening to her box, and Sherlock's happy bark was loud. She grinned and opened the door and her arms. Her puppy leaped up and licked her face. She hugged him. "Good boy!"

Her muscles were stiff as she crawled out and stood shivering in the wind gusting off Lake Superior. Another siren wailed in the distance. Bree Matthews, the owner of Kitchigami Search-and-Rescue Training Center, gave her a thumbs-up. Bree was Naomi's best friend and one of the coolest adults ever. Emily wanted to be just like Bree when she grew up.

Smiling, Emily joined Bree and Samson, Bree's world-renowned search dog. "Sherlock is learning fast."

"He sure is." Bree glanced at her watch. "It's nearly five, so I think we're about done for the day."

"Aw, do we have to quit? If I go home, I'll just have to do homework."

"I thought you liked school."

"I do, but I'd rather train Sherlock. There's the competition coming up."

"Ah, the competition." Bree's green eyes were smiling. "I should have known you'd have that in mind. Okay, we can run them through the obstacle course one more time." She motioned to the other students, all older than Emily, to move to the obstacle course.

The competition for SAR dogs in training was only three weeks away, and Emily thought Sherlock just might win his division. He was young, sure, but he was so smart. Her puppy was a born search dog.

She led Sherlock to the beginning of the obstacles. The course was made of tire swings, a log beam, a teeter-totter kind of board that the dogs had to walk up and down, a large wooden structure that had an open window in it, and boulders.

"I'll have Samson go first." Bree snapped her fingers, and Samson took off.

Emily watched in awe as Samson leaped onto the very top of the wooden structure, not even bothering to brace his hind legs on the windowsill. He bounded down on the other side, then ran toward the tire swing. The thing barely moved as he launched himself through the opening. He leaped onto the log beam and walked it without flinching. It was so cool.

"See that, Sherlock? You'll be able to do that someday," she whispered into her puppy's ear and scratched his chin.

When Samson finished the obstacle course, everyone clapped, and he trotted back toward them with his curly tail held high. What a ham. She patted Samson's head as he passed.

"Your turn, Sherlock." She led her dog into position. "Jump!" She pointed at the fake wall structure. Her puppy whined and pressed his head against her leg.

"Come on, boy, you can do it." She pointed and gave him the order again. He lay down at her feet and regarded her with sad eyes.

Emily's heart fell to her feet. She glanced at Bree. "I don't understand. He did okay the last time."

"He fell though, remember? Walk him through it with the leash."

"He hates that."

"You have to help him get over his fear." Bree's tone left no room for argument.

Sighing, Emily clipped the lead to his collar and tugged him forward. He came with lagging feet. "Come on, boy." She coaxed the puppy to the wall and helped him inch to the ledge, where he perched for a few moments before leaping through to the other side.

She dropped the leash and clapped. "You did it, Sherlock!"

Bree and the class members clapped, and Sherlock barked

and ran in circles around Emily's legs, tangling her in his leash. She dropped to her knees and hugged him. "You'll figure it out, Sherlock. Good dog!" His tail wagged his whole body.

Her grin faded when something moved in the woods to her left. She squinted in the bright sunshine, then gasped when she caught a glimpse of a woman standing in the shadows. *Marika?* Emily's heart raced faster than Samson on the course. She stared harder, standing up, but the figure melted into the darkness of the thick forest.

It couldn't have been Marika, could it? Dad and Naomi said Sheriff Kaleva had found no trace of her in Rock Harbor. Emily bit her lip and swallowed hard. She was probably just seeing things. She stepped forward, wanting to make sure.

As she approached the edge of the trees, some shrubs parted and her mother stepped into the light. "Hello, sweetheart."

Emily backed away. "What are you doing here?"

Marika was as beautiful as ever, with her long dark hair and compelling eyes. "I wanted to see you, of course. I'm still your mother. I do love you, even if you don't believe it."

"Just like you loved Timmy so much that you messed with his insulin meds?" The words burst out of Emily before she could stop them.

Marika's lips tightened. "It wasn't what you think."

"It never is, is it?" She scooped up Sherlock and held him tight for courage.

"I want to be in your life, Emily. Your father will agree to it if you ask him."

Emily bit her lip. Her mother had always been persuasive, and even now, Emily wished she could believe her. Sherlock squirmed in her arms when someone shouted his name.

"I have to go. Think about it, Emily. I'll be in touch." Marika turned around and hurried into the recesses of the trees.

Her mouth dry, Emily stared after her. What was she supposed to do? Her dad had always told her it was important to forgive, but if she did, did that mean she had to see Marika? Shuddering, she began to retrace her steps to join the rest of the group.

God, I don't know if I can forgive Marika. A mother is supposed to always love her children and take care of them, right? She didn't. Emily let out a heavy breath. This was so hard. *God, I'd really appreciate some help in forgiving her because I really, really don't want to.*

Her cell phone vibrated in her pocket. She jumped and then pulled it out. Waiting for her mother to show up was just making her jumpy. She blinked at the message and read it again.

call me. fire at the school.

A fire? She put her hand to her mouth and shuddered, forgetting about Marika for the moment.

Bree moved beside her. "What's wrong?"

"I just got a text message. There's been a fire at the school." Emily punched in Olivia's number. The class murmured and gathered around her as the call began to ring through. Several people dug in their pockets for their cell phones.

"Hello?" Olivia's voice sounded strained.

"I just got your message, Liv. Is everyone okay?"

"Oh, Em, it's terrible! You should see the lab. It's all black and burned. I bet it's going to take weeks to rebuild it. I don't know for sure if anyone is hurt or not. The medical team of the fire department has been giving oxygen to a few people, but I just don't know."

"An explosion?" Emily could see it in her mind's eye. Some of the other kids liked mixing things that didn't go together. "Was anyone hurt?" At least Timmy and Dave were playing in the SAR building.

"No one seems to know right now. You should get over here though. There are fire trucks everywhere, and practically the whole town is pitching in to help. Your dad and Naomi are here with my parents."

"On my way." Emily ended the call and glanced around at her classmates. "She doesn't know if anyone was hurt."

"My son was there this afternoon for football practice," Mrs. Wilson said. "I have to get over there. Emily, can you take charge of my dog and drop him by my house?"

Emily opened her mouth to refuse but then saw the panic in her face. "Sure. I'll put him in the fence behind the house." It was only a few blocks out of her way to the school.

Several other people asked her to do the same so they could check on their kids. Emily had four dogs on leads by the time she left the training center, plus Sherlock.

God, please don't let anyone be hurt.

THREE

Lights on top of the fire truck and police cars cast creepy shadows over the school. Smoke hung like clouds in the late afternoon air. Fire hoses spread out over the school grounds like a weird spiderweb. Emily dodged two firemen jogging across the parking lot as she dialed Olivia's number. The stench burned her nose.

Olivia barely had time to answer before Emily interrupted. "Where are you?"

"Are you here?"

"Yes, just got here. I can't find you though. There are so many people."

"Come to the gym. The teachers and Mayor Kaleva have set up a kind of headquarters here. Mom and Dad are handing out bottles of water. Your dad is helping replace the firemen's tools as needed, and Naomi is helping keep the little kids occupied. I'll let Naomi know you got here okay."

"On my way to you." Emily slipped her cell phone back into her pocket and headed for Olivia. She sidestepped two sheriff deputies who nearly ran over her. Everyone had turned out to help in this town emergency, no matter what his or her job.

"Emily! Emily O'Reilly."

She turned to find Inetta Harris rushing toward her. Inetta was a pretty woman, with long, auburn hair, probably in her forties or so. She'd proven herself to be Emily and Olivia's friend—even if she had been friends with Marika in high school.

"Isn't this awful?" Inetta asked as she stood beside Emily.

"What happened?" Emily knew Inetta would have already asked the fire chief and Sheriff Kaleva for details. She was, after all, Rock Harbor's only reporter.

"According to Chief Dix, the fire started in the high school science lab."

Emily walked slowly toward the gym. "Were kids messing around and mixing stuff?" She'd sure hate to be them right now.

"According to Principal Sturgeon, no one was supposed to be in the school. Football practice was on the field, and band practice was in the stands."

"So what happened?"

"Sheriff Kaleva is still talking with the fire department, but right now, their best estimation is someone broke into the lab and started a fire."

Emily stopped and twisted to stare at Inetta. "On purpose?"

"Too early to say." Inetta grabbed Emily's arm just in time to pull her out of the way as a hose was rolled out across their path. "Are your folks here? You shouldn't be out alone. It's dangerous."

"Olivia said everyone's by the gym." *So that's why the cops were here too.*

Nodding, Inetta led the way. "The mayor's had the radio station ask people to stay home, but if they were missing children or family members, to come to the gym."

"Hey, I need to ask a favor later."

"What?"

Emily shook her head. "Nothing urgent. This is more important at the moment." She waved her hand across the area.

It was crazy. In just the short time Emily had been there, the crowd had grown. People were everywhere . . . crying, calling out names, and being told to go to the gym. It was so loud. Emily wanted to cover her ears to block it all out.

They passed through an area still congested with heavy, black smoke. Not only did Emily's nose burn, but her eyes started to water. She blinked, letting Inetta guide her. She turned her head away from the school and smoke. People stood behind the fire trucks and stared. Some had their hands over their mouths. Others just wore shocked expressions. A man with smudges on his face hugged a woman. A lady held a crying toddler. A woman—

And there she was . . . Marika.

Emily froze and widened her eyes as her birth mother made eye contact and smiled. Just for a split second, then Marika was gone. Emily blinked and shook her head, but she couldn't see her anymore. Not behind the line of people.

"What's wrong?" Inetta tugged on her arm.

"Did you see her?"

Inetta followed Emily's line of vision and peered into the crowd. "See who?"

"Marika." But she didn't see her anymore.

Inetta's gaze shot across the people standing by the emergency vehicles. "Marika? You see her? Where?"

"She's gone now."

Inetta turned Emily to face her. "Are you sure it was her?"

Chewing her bottom lip, Emily glanced back to the crowd. Her eyes were burning. She'd been blinking, so her vision was a little blurry.

"Emily, are you sure you saw your mother?"

She didn't see any sign of her. Maybe she'd been mistaken? "I—I don't know. I thought I did. I mean, she looked right at me. And I saw her earlier today. She talked to me then." But then she'd disappeared. Wouldn't Marika have come up to her? That's what she'd threatened to do—to come take Emily and Timmy.

Inetta put an arm around her shoulders and steered her toward the gym. "There are a lot of people here. It's smoky and crowded. Lots of things happening all at once. Easy enough to have your eyes play tricks on you."

"Yeah. I guess so." Emily glanced over her shoulder. Still no sign of Marika. She could have gotten here though. It had taken forever for Emily to deliver all the search dogs to their homes. She shivered.

"It happens to us all. Understandably so right now." Inetta stopped outside the gym door. "Here we are. You go on ahead and find your folks. I have to hunt down Chief Dix and see what I can find out."

"Thanks, Inetta." Emily took a step, then turned back to Inetta. "Let me know what you find out, okay?"

Inetta arched a single eyebrow. "Why?"

"Just curious, I guess." Emily shrugged.

Inetta chuckled. "With your sense of curiosity, I just might turn you into a reporter yet."

Emily smiled as she entered the gym. Maybe her curiosity and sense of wanting to solve a mystery were why she wanted herself and Sherlock to be the best SAR team after Bree and Samson.

"There you are." Olivia met her just inside the doorway. "I was getting worried about you. What took you so long?"

They walked in the gym right in front of Josh Thorensen, Trevor Bray, and Caycie Nelson, all high school members of the school's surf team. Emily still thought Josh was way cute with his thick hair, blue eyes, and lean build, but he acted like she didn't exist. That was okay . . . she was only fourteen, and right now, everything in her life seemed to be upside down. And now this fire.

"It's crowded out there, and I ran into Inetta," Emily explained. "Did you know they think someone broke into the science lab and that's where the fire started?" She fell into step beside Olivia.

"I heard one of the teachers say they thought it was set on purpose," Caycie interrupted. She'd been walking close enough to hear Emily and Olivia. She tossed her hair over her shoulder. "Who would try to burn down our school?"

Trevor held Caycie's hand. "Good thing no one was here."

The gym was crowded with people, maybe even more than outside. In one corner, tables were set up with coffee urns and ice chests full of water. Across the gym, there were tables with two big dry-erase boards. Emily recognized several teachers writing and erasing names.

Olivia turned to Emily. "Did Inetta say who?"

Emily shook her head. "But she's been talking with Sheriff Kaleva, and she promised to let me know when she knew something."

Caycie shook her head. "This is just crazy."

Josh glanced at the cell phone he held. "Hey, Coach Larson is looking for us. We're supposed to meet him by the drink machine."

"Emily, let me know if you hear anything else, okay? If someone did try to burn down our school, what's to stop them from trying again?" Caycie shivered.

"I'll protect you," Trevor said as he flexed his muscles.

Josh laughed and mock-punched Trevor in the gut. "Come on, before Coach blows a gasket."

With a weak smile, Caycie left with Josh and Trevor.

"Wow." Olivia pulled her toward the bleachers. They found a small space on the front row and crammed together. "I just can't believe all this. It has to be an accident."

Emily pulled out her cell phone. She quickly typed out a text to her dad and Naomi to let them know she was safe in the gym, then returned the phone to her pocket. "No one was supposed to be in the science lab. Just someone being there is bad."

"May I have your attention, please? Everyone?" Mayor Hilary Kaleva spoke into a bullhorn. The entire gym grew quiet, except for a little kid or two crying. "Thank you. I wanted to give everyone an update. If you've just joined us, please check the name board over in the corner. A few teens still haven't checked in, and the parents are very worried."

Three of the varsity football players lingering around the doorway shuffled toward the corner.

The bullhorn screeched. "Rock Harbor's fire department has concluded with putting out the fire but will stay to ensure it doesn't rekindle."

Applause burst out throughout the gym.

Mayor Kaleva nodded, then continued, "Yes, we're certainly thankful for their heroic work. However, since the cause of the fire is under investigation, Fire Chief Jack Dix has requested to speak with everyone prior to your leaving. He and his team are stationed by the doors and will need to get some information from each of you before you leave. Thank you for your cooperation."

The mayor's last words were drowned out with people talking and lots of people heading to the doors. There were way too many trying to move to the same place at the same time, crowding and pushing. Emily felt as if the air had been sucked from the gym.

"Come on." Emily grabbed Olivia's hand and headed up the bleachers. "Let's look for our parents."

She'd barely reached the top row when she saw her father pointing up at her, Naomi holding Matthew, Emily's baby brother, tightly in hand, standing beside him. Emily and Olivia made their way back down the bleachers. Dad pulled Emily into a big bear hug. "Hi, honey. I'm so glad you and Timmy were at Bree's when the fire broke out. I would have been worried sick."

Even though she'd just turned fourteen, she loved having Dad hold her. It made her feel so safe. "Do they know what happened yet?"

"We don't know." Naomi put Matthew's hand in Dad's, then gave Emily a hug as well. "Mason said the chief has called in the arson investigator."

"Arson?" Emily locked gazes with Olivia.

"That's not certain yet, Em. They're just looking into it." Dad hoisted Matthew to his shoulder.

"Olivia! Are you ready to head home?" Mrs. Webster joined the group. "Your father went to get the car." She smiled weakly at Naomi. "This is just awful. I'm so glad none of the children were here."

Naomi nodded. "I know. I can't even imagine how long it'll take to rebuild that part of the school."

"Will we still have school?" Emily caught her tongue between her teeth. If school was closed, even for a couple of days, the History Smackdown team wouldn't be ready for their first meet. They were on a winning streak.

"Yes, you'll still have school." Mrs. Webster grinned. "But I'm sure there will be some rearranging of some classes. The news should have more information tonight."

"Come on, Olivia." She gave a nod to the O'Reilly family.

"Call me later," Olivia mouthed at Emily as she followed her mother toward the gym door. In minutes, the crowd of people swallowed them up and hid them from Emily's sight.

"Speaking of getting home, we need to get this one home for dinner." Dad tickled Matthew, causing him to giggle, then set him on the ground, but he kept a firm hold on his hand. Matthew was famous for breaking free from parental containment.

"I'm hungry," Matthew wailed on cue.

Naomi chuckled and put her arm around Emily's shoulders. "Your dad and I are in separate cars. What do you say we let them head home and start dinner, and you and I run by Bree's and pick up Timmy?"

"What?" Dad wore wide eyes. "I have to start dinner? All by myself?"

"I'll help you, Daddy." Matthew jumped up and down in place. Everyone laughed.

"Then Matthew and I will get things started." He leaned over and gave both Emily and Naomi a kiss on the cheek. "But don't be too long, or you might not recognize the kitchen when you get back."

"We'll be quick." Naomi took hold of Emily's hand. "We're parked closer to this door." They went to the door opposite of the one Dad and Matthew had gone toward.

Sheriff Kaleva stood beside Chief Dix. He gave Naomi a stiff smile. She reached out and squeezed his forearm. "Mason, this is so awful. Can I do anything more to help?"

He shook his head. "Hilary's already working on getting a rebuilding fund-raiser organized. I'm sure she'll be calling you about that soon."

"It's so awful."

He lifted his notepad and scribbled their names. "Were either of you here when the fire broke out?"

"No. I'd just dropped off some donations to the animal shelter when I saw the smoke. I came right over. The fire truck was already here by the time I'd parked."

He finished writing, then looked at Emily. "What about you?"

She shook her head. "I was at the SAR school working with Sherlock."

He smiled. "Bree tells us that puppy of yours has great potential."

"Really?" It was one thing for Bree to tell Emily Sherlock had promise . . . it was something else for her to tell the sheriff and mayor—even if they were Bree's family.

"Sure. She said with continued training, he could one day surpass Charley."

"Hey now." Naomi rose to her dog's defense, but she smiled. "Sherlock does have great potential." She hugged Emily. "And Emily's turning out to be a great handler."

Heat shot to Emily's cheeks as the sheriff moved them through the door so he could speak to the man behind them.

Emily's feet barely touched the ground as she walked with

Naomi to the SUV. Bree and Naomi both thought she was good—she couldn't wait to tell Olivia.

"Naomi O'Reilly!" a woman's voice yelled over the parking lot.

Both Emily and Naomi turned to find a woman in one of the tight uniforms from the Copper Club marching over the asphalt. "We don't need your charity. Or any of your religious mumbo jumbo."

Even in the dark, Emily could see Naomi's face turning red.

Naomi shifted, stepping in front of Emily. "Odetta, isn't it?"

"What's it to you, Ms. High and Mighty?"

"The breads and cookies weren't charity. They were just some things for you and the other waitresses to enjoy. And there was no judgment, religious or otherwise."

"Well, we didn't need the cards with Scripture on them, and we don't need your food. You aren't any better than any of us. We're doing honest work to earn an honest living. Just because you Holy Rollers think the club is a den of sin doesn't mean that we're all bad."

"No one ever said that, Odetta."

The waitress glared at her. "Just stay away from us. We don't want or need anything from you." She turned and marched off.

"What was that all about?" Emily asked.

"Just someone who misread a nice gesture. It's nothing." Naomi shook her head. "Come on, your dad's probably already made a huge mess in the kitchen."

Emily smiled and buckled her seat belt, but her mind couldn't forget Odetta's face. It'd been pinched and looked like she was ready to throw a punch.

It kind of scared Emily.

 **FOUR**

"I can't believe how cold it's gotten so fast." Naomi stepped out of the SUV and wound her scarf around her neck.

Emily tightened her jacket. Good thing she'd remembered to grab it when she'd taken Sherlock home after the training session. The wind off the lake could chill to the bone quickly.

Naomi knocked on the front door of Bree and Kade's lighthouse. Emily absolutely adored their home. She loved how old it was, how the wood floors squeaked when she stepped on them, and how the sun slanted through the wavy glass in the windows. One day, she wanted to have a home with as much character as the lighthouse.

"Hey." Kade opened the door. "Come on in." He shut the door behind them. "Wow, the temperature's really dropping out there."

Emily could easily see why Bree had married Kade. He was tall like Dad with dark brown hair and pretty blue eyes, but what made him really hot was how nice he was. As a park ranger, he cared a lot about animals and taking care of them. And besides, he never treated her like she was just a kid like some adults did.

Naomi set her scarf on the entry table. "Sorry I'm so late getting Timmy, but with the fire . . ."

Kade smiled. "Please. You know Timmy's no bother. He keeps Dave out of trouble when he's here."

Bree joined them in the living room, both of the twins trailing after her. "Is there any more news?"

Naomi shook her head. "Just that Principal Sturgeon is positive no one was supposed to be in the lab."

Hannah and Hunter, both precious three-year-olds, caught sight of Emily and ran toward her, squealing. She knelt to accept their hugs and kisses. She babysat them as often as she could to make spending money, but it never felt like work because she loved them so much.

"Is it possible someone left something on in the lab at the end of school and it took a few hours for a fire to start?" Kade asked.

"I don't know." Naomi leaned her hip against the back of the couch. "Mason and Jack Dix were asking everyone questions as they left. Maybe they'll get some sort of lead. I guess they'll be able to tell more once they've secured the school."

Timmy and Dave exploded into the room. "Mom, can Dave spend the night with me? Please? We'll go to bed as soon as you say."

"Not tonight, sport," Kade answered before Naomi could. "It's a school night."

"But we'll go to bed on time. We promise." Emily's little brother gave Naomi what she'd dubbed "the puppy dog eyes."

Naomi didn't budge. "Maybe you boys can have a sleepover this weekend, after the homecoming celebration." She ran a hand over his hair, messing it up. "Go get your stuff. We left Dad and Matthew alone in the kitchen to start dinner."

"That could be a disaster." Bree chuckled. "Go help Timmy get his things, Dave."

The boys headed down the hall, moving much slower than they'd entered. Hannah and Hunter trotted behind them, mumbling in their toddler twin-talk.

Emily stood and shoved her hands in her pockets. "Inetta Harris said Sheriff Kaleva thought someone broke into the lab and started a fire."

"Really?" Naomi turned to stare at her. "I didn't hear that."

"She said nothing was sure yet, though." Oh man. She hoped she hadn't gotten Inetta in trouble by saying anything. Inetta hadn't said she shouldn't say anything. Maybe she should just stop talking.

"I ran into Odetta Sayers in the parking lot. Or rather, she ran into me." Naomi locked stares with Bree.

"And?" Bree raised her eyebrows.

"Let's just say we probably shouldn't deliver any more food to the Copper Club." Naomi tilted her head toward Emily.

Really? Did they think she didn't notice? She was fourteen, after all, not some little kid who couldn't understand things.

Before anyone could comment further, Bree's cell phone rang. She yanked it from her pocket. "Hello?"

Timmy and Dave returned, being loud and just, well, boys. Kade shushed them as he scooped Hannah and Hunter up into his arms. The twins giggled as he jostled them and made silly faces.

"I see." Bree wore a frown, which usually meant only one thing . . .

A search and rescue.

"It's okay. Naomi's here with me. We'll meet you there." Bree slipped the phone into her back pocket.

"Somebody missing?" Naomi stiffened.

"Just a search. Mason found some fabric of what appears to be a fleece jacket that was caught in the hallway's main door. He believes it might be from the person who broke into the school. He asked the dogs to come see what they can sniff out."

"Let me drop the kids off with Donovan, and I'll grab Charley and meet you at the school." Naomi turned to Timmy. "Let's go, buddy."

Timmy opened the front door, gave Dave a knuckle bump, then jumped to the ground, skipping the steps. Naomi followed.

Emily's muscles tensed. "Can I come?"

Naomi glanced back over her shoulder. "Honey, this isn't a search and rescue. This is looking for a clue. It's not nearly as exciting as you might think."

"I want to come—even if it's boring. It would be great training for Sherlock." She held her breath as Naomi looked at Bree.

"Why not?" Bree shrugged. "We can always use another set of eyes and hands."

Emily forced herself not to jump up and down.

Naomi grinned. "Well, come on. We'll get the dogs and meet you there, Bree."

Bounding down the stairs, Emily pressed her lips together to stop from shouting out. She climbed into the SUV and latched her seat belt, excitement exploding inside her chest. This would be a great search. Especially since no one was lost or hurt. They'd just be hunting down clues.

Speaking of hunting down clues, Emily sent a quick text to Inetta, asking the reporter to meet her and Olivia after school tomorrow. They'd share a *panukakkua* or *pulla* and tell Inetta about Olivia being adopted and about what Emily found on the

Internet. She'd be able to help. And there could always be an e-mail response waiting already.

Inetta replied immediately that she'd see them at the Suomi Café tomorrow afternoon.

Emily shoved her phone into her jacket pocket. Maybe she'd have even more to share with Inetta tomorrow. After all, she was on her way to a real search to solve a serious crime!

The sharp scent of smoke still hung in the air of the school yard and choked Emily's throat. She kept a tight hold on the leashes as she followed Bree and Naomi toward the front entrance of the school. The crowd was gone, but the turf was trampled from all the feet.

The sheriff's stocky form filled the doorway as he stepped out to meet them. His face was somber and streaked with soot. Something about the whole scene made Emily jumpy. It was starting to get dark, and she imagined she saw shadows moving inside the school. Probably deputies and firemen, but it was still pretty creepy. She bent down and scratched Charley's ears and immediately felt a little better. Nothing could happen to her with the dogs here.

Bree stopped in front of him. "You found something, Mason?"

He handed her a paper bag. "I used gloves to put it in here. This scrap of fabric was caught on the latch of the door. Someone was in a hurry coming out and got caught. It's navy fleece. Might have come from a jacket or a sweatshirt."

"Show me where it was found," Bree said. "I want to see if there's anything else."

Emily straightened Sherlock's leash and grabbed the ready-kit backpack, fully outfitted with a first-aid kit, small plastic tarp, energy bars, flashlight, flares, bug repellant, towelettes, compass, Swiss Army knife, radio, topographic map of the area, canteen, sunglasses, sunscreen, and every other item anyone could need on a search. They probably wouldn't need any of that searching around the school, but the first rule of search and rescue was to always be prepared.

The sheriff's bushy brows rose when he glanced at her, then he locked stares with Naomi. "You're letting her search with you? I'm not so sure she needs to see inside. It might be traumatic for a kid."

Emily drew herself up. "I'm old enough to help. Sherlock has a good nose, and I've helped with Charley too. You know the dogs do a good job together." She took courage from her own words. There was nothing to fear inside the school.

He glanced at Bree, who nodded. "I want to keep it cordoned off until my detectives are through. Just see what you can do with this fabric."

"All right." Bree knelt by the dogs, then opened the bag. She let Samson sniff first, then thrust the open bag under Charley's nose. Sherlock was the last to sniff. Emily unsnapped the leashes.

"Search, Samson!" Bree gave the order.

Samson's curly tail wagged. He ran out to the opening by the flagpole. His nose in the air, he darted across the grass, then back the other way. Charley followed him, and so did Sherlock. Emily watched her puppy closely as he sniffed the grass, then lifted his leg at the flagpole. Samson and Charley ignored him, crisscrossing the area with their noses in the air.

"No, Sherlock!" Emily's face burned, and she started toward him.

"Let him alone. He'll figure it out," Bree said.

Naomi grabbed Emily's arm. "They all have to learn. He's just a puppy, remember. Give him time."

The puppy nosed along a row of mums, then barked excitedly and chased a rabbit from the plants. Emily sighed. He didn't seem to understand he was supposed to be working.

Naomi's grip on Emily's arm tightened. "Samson has a scent!"

Samson's tail went up, and he barked. He raced around the corner of the school with Charley on his heels. Sherlock yipped and ran after them, but it was clear the puppy didn't want to be left out of whatever new adventure his friends had found. Emily stuffed the leashes in the pockets of her jacket as she chased the dogs. Samson veered to go around to the back of the school, and Charley followed. Sherlock, on the other hand, went in the opposite direction.

Emily's lungs burned as she put on an extra burst of speed to grab her puppy, then follow Bree and Naomi, who had followed the big dogs. At the back of the building, Samson had leaped up against the door and barked. Charley had his feet planted and barked ferociously as well. Emily set Sherlock on the ground, and he promptly went to nose the dirt under the window.

Bree reached the door and grabbed Samson's collar. "Easy, boy."

When Emily reached the door, she bent over and dragged in a few deep breaths before she could speak. "Why would they come back here when the front door was open? I think the dogs got derailed."

Bree shook her head. "Look at Samson and Charley. They still have the scent."

"Part of being a good SAR team is to know your dog's behavior. That means observing them." Naomi tugged on the door. "Locked. Where does this lead?"

"To the football locker room, I think," Emily said. Not that she'd ever been inside it. Sweaty boys . . . gross.

The sheriff reached them. The big man was huffing. "I have a key." He dug in his pocket and pulled out a key. After an initial fumble, he got it unlocked.

The acrid stench of smoke rushed out, and Emily took an involuntary step back. The sheriff waved his hand in the air. Even this far from the actual fire, it stunk.

Bree didn't seem to mind the smell. She released Samson's collar, and the dog darted into the dark hall. Bree and Naomi followed.

Emily hung back. "Got a flashlight? It's dark in there. I don't want Sherlock to get cut."

The sheriff grinned and reached inside to flip the switch. "We have power."

The light helped Emily step inside. There was water everywhere. And leaves dragged in by the water hoses covered the floor. The walls were marred too. "I guess they brought the hoses in everywhere they could."

She couldn't see Bree or Naomi, but around the corner, Samson began to bark. Charley nearly tripped her up as he ran after Samson.

"I think he's found something." Emily let Sherlock ahead as she followed the noise.

She found Naomi and Bree standing in the boys' locker room. It felt weird to be where girls weren't supposed to be. Lockers lined the walls, and there was a heap of shoulder pads on the bench at the back wall. Emily wrinkled her nose at the smell under the scent of smoke. It smelled like old shoes. She forced her attention back to Bree.

"Found it." Bree pointed to a fleece jacket on the floor. "I haven't touched it."

The sheriff pulled a pair of gloves from his pocket and slipped them on. Kneeling by the jacket, he lifted one sleeve, then the other. When he found nothing, he flipped the jacket over. "Ah, this is the one. There's a piece missing at the waist. I'll run it through forensics and see if we can find anything."

Emily stared hard at the jacket. Where had she seen it before?

FIVE

"Charley's acting funny," Timmy announced as he plopped into his chair at the kitchen table. He grabbed Emily's glass of chocolate milk.

"Hey, that's mine." Emily took her glass back. "Get your own." But she passed him the chocolate mix before putting her empty plate in the dishwasher and opening the back door to let Sherlock out into the fenced yard.

Sunlight pushed through the trees heavy with red and yellow leaves, casting shadows on the ground. Sherlock chased the blowing leaves, growling and barking. Emily grinned at her puppy as she made sure he and Charley had water in their outside bowls. "Hey, are we having school today?"

"According to the news, yes. Principal Sturgeon said some of the high school classes would be held in the junior high wings, but that he would hold an assembly first thing this morning." Dad took another sip of his coffee.

"Charley's acting funny?" Naomi turned from the stove, still holding the spatula tipped with pancake batter. "How?"

43

Timmy dumped two large tablespoons of chocolate mix into his glass of milk. "He was twitching around and wouldn't come downstairs with me."

"Emily, will you watch this pancake for me, please?" Naomi flipped the pancake, handed Emily the spatula, and rushed up the stairs.

"What do you mean by 'twitching around'?" Emily asked Timmy.

"I dunno." Timmy shrugged. "Like his feet sometimes do when he's sleeping and dreaming of chasing a squirrel, only it was kinda his whole body and he wasn't asleep."

Her mouth went dry as she locked stares with her father. That did not sound good.

"I'm sure he's fine, honey." But Dad looked worried himself as he took a sip of coffee. "Don't let the pancake burn."

Emily scooped it up and slid it onto a plate that she handed to Timmy. She made sure to turn off the stove and move the griddle to the back burner.

"Donovan!" The fear in Naomi's voice carried down the stairs.

Dad kicked back his chair, nearly knocking it over, and rushed out of the room. Emily's heart pounded. "Stay here with Matthew," she told Timmy before running to the stairs.

In the hallway, Dad had his cell to his ear as he kept a hand on Naomi's shoulder. Naomi knelt alongside Charley just outside Timmy's room. Charley wasn't shaking or anything as Emily approached, so that had to be good. Right? The smell indicated he'd peed on the floor. And he was drooling as Naomi used a tissue to wipe around his eyes, which when he stared up at Emily, looked so sad.

"What's wrong with him?"

"I don't know. Dad's talking to Dr. Meeks right now." Naomi stroked his head. He leaned against her.

"But he's going to be all fine, right?" Emily couldn't imagine something being *bad* wrong with him.

Naomi's eyes were shiny with tears as she shrugged. "We'll have to wait to hear what Dr. Meeks says, but we should pray."

Emily nodded. *Dear God, please don't let anything really bad be wrong with Charley. We all love him so much.* She couldn't imagine how she'd feel if it were Sherlock, and Naomi had owned Charley long before she married Dad.

Dad put his cell in his pocket. "Dr. Meeks said to bring Charley in now. He'll meet you there."

Naomi pressed her lips together until white ringed them, and she nodded, but she kept petting Charley's head.

"I'll get him in the SUV. Don't worry about the kids. We'll get everyone where they're supposed to be, right, Em?" Dad turned to her and gave her big eyes, clearly urging her to reassure Naomi.

"Right. I'll get the boys ready and make sure they have their backpacks and lunches."

Naomi stood, and Dad gently lifted Charley in his arms. They went down the stairs together, Emily following.

Timmy met them in the foyer with Matthew right behind him. "What's wrong with Charley?" His voice cracked. "Is he gonna be okay?"

Emily wrapped an arm around his shoulders and pulled him in for a sideways hug. "He's going to see Dr. Meeks. You know what great care Dr. Meeks takes of Charley."

"So he'll be okay?" Timmy's eyes looked as sad as Charley's had.

"I'm praying he'll be just fine."

"I'll pray too."

Naomi turned and kissed all three of them, grabbed her purse from the table in the entry, and then followed Dad outside.

Lord, please keep watch over Charley. Let him be okay. Please.

She let out a heavy sigh and let go of Timmy. "Come on, let's get ready for school. Dad's going to take us."

"Think he'll let us listen to sports talk on the way to school?" Timmy headed to the stairs without waiting for an answer.

"Take Matthew with you. Make sure he brushes his teeth." Emily smiled at her baby brother, who seemed more than happy to trail Timmy. He followed his brother everywhere, trying to copy everything Timmy did or said.

"Hey, Timmy," Emily called up the stairs after them. "Charley had an accident in the hallway. Please stay away from it until I can get it cleaned up. And keep Matthew out of it too, please."

"Okay."

Emily put all the dirty dishes into the dishwasher and had just finished pushing the chairs up to the table when Dad came back. She leaned against the counter. "I turned off the coffeepot. I figured you were done with it. The boys are upstairs brushing their teeth."

"Thanks, sweetheart."

She reached into the supply cabinet and pulled out the pine cleaner.

"What are you doing with that?"

"Charley's accident upstairs. I don't think Naomi had time to disinfect the area."

"You don't have to do that, honey. I'll get it." Dad reached for the cleaning bottle.

Emily took a step back. "No, it's fine. I just want to get it done so Naomi doesn't have to do it when she gets back."

"Well, thank you. It's very considerate."

She turned to head to the stairs, then paused. "Dad, is Charley going to be okay?"

"Dr. Meeks said he'd probably have to run some tests to find out what's wrong, then he'll be able to figure out a treatment plan."

"But he'll be okay?"

Dad paused, and Emily's heart hiccuped. "I don't know, honey. I hope so. I'm praying so. But I honestly don't know yet."

She nodded and headed up the stairs. On one hand, it was great her dad trusted her enough to tell her the truth, but on the other, it was rough because it meant she knew the situation with Charley was serious—serious enough that Naomi and Dad were worried.

And that meant she was worried too.

"You don't know any more than that?" Olivia stared at Emily.

Emily shook her head. As more students filled the bleachers in the gym, she leaned closer to Olivia so others couldn't hear their conversation. "We packed up the dogs and left right after that, so I have no idea what the sheriff did with the jacket, but I know I've seen it somewhere before. I just can't remember who I saw wearing it." She shivered. "And then for Charley to be so sick this morning . . . well, I don't even know what to think."

"That's a little freaky. I—"

"Everybody take a seat and quiet down." Principal Sturgeon's voice boomed over the speakers in the school's gym.

All the high school and junior high students went still and silent. The bleachers were filled, kids squished together. Emily could make out Caycie and Trevor two rows in front of her.

"Thank you." The principal pulled the microphone from the holder and began to pace. "As I'm sure you're all aware, we'll be moving some of the classes that had rooms damaged by last night's fire. Any classrooms in the east wing of the science lab will be moved. A full listing of new class locations will be handed out by Ms. Bridges as you leave the assembly."

Whispers grew louder from the bleachers, as did individual voices. Caycie turned around and caught Emily's eye. *Have you heard anything?* she mouthed.

Emily shook her head.

Caycie turned back around.

"Excuse me." Principal Sturgeon waited until everyone had quieted down again. "Sheriff Kaleva and Fire Chief Dix have taped off areas with yellow caution tape. No one, and I mean *no one*, is to cross into those areas. Anyone who does will receive immediate suspension."

Mumblings came from the upper row of bleachers where the seniors sat.

"This is not up for discussion, students. Do I make myself clear?"

A chorus of "yes" and "okay" and a couple of "yes, sirs" filled the air. Principal Sturgeon nodded. "If you'll give your attention to Sheriff Kaleva, he has an announcement."

Emily hadn't noticed him standing among the gathered teachers on the gym floor, but he stepped up and took the microphone from the principal. He set a duffel bag on the floor beside him. "Hello, students. I'm very sorry for the damage to your school, but rest assured we're looking into what caused the fire."

Only a few boys in the back made noise, and those were only clearing their throats and coughing.

"We know a person or persons broke into the science lab where the fire started. It could have been a prank. The fire could have been an accident. We understand these things can happen." The sheriff let his words sink in for a minute. "But we need to know what happened, and that's why I'm here today. To ask for your help."

He opened the duffel and pulled out a clear bag holding the blue fleece jacket they'd found in the locker room last night.

Emily grabbed Olivia's hand. "That's the one Samson found," she whispered.

"We have reason to believe the person who broke into the science lab was wearing this jacket. We are asking the person who owns it to come forward and answer a few questions." He walked across the bleachers, holding up the bag with the jacket.

The room went as silent as Emily had ever heard.

"You don't have to come right this minute, but I'll be in the office for about thirty minutes after the assembly. If this is your jacket, or you know whose it is, please report to the office right after you are dismissed. Thank you." The sheriff handed the microphone back to Principal Sturgeon and put the jacket back into the duffel. He left the gym without another word.

"Students, I feel sure the owner of the jacket will report to the office immediately after the assembly. However, I've made the decision that if no one does come forward to claim the jacket, or no one with information about the jacket comes forward, I'll have no choice but to cancel the homecoming celebration this weekend."

Everyone seemed to speak at once. Students loudly protested the principal's ruling. Others began to talk and whisper to each other.

"Excuse me," Principal Sturgeon spoke loudly into the microphone. "I hope it doesn't come to that, but that's the choice of the owner of the jacket and his friends." He paused as people continued to mumble, although not as loudly. "Don't forget to get the new class location and schedule from Ms. Bridges as you leave. You are dismissed. Please report to your second-period class."

The gym erupted in noise as everyone got up and headed down the bleachers to go to class.

"I can't believe it. Cancel the homecoming celebration?" Olivia stood, shaking her head.

"I know." Emily couldn't believe it herself. "It's so unfair. The whole town gets involved—not just us kids."

Olivia shifted her backpack as they made their way down the bleachers. "Yeah. Dad's been helping the committee with some of the booths. They just finished all the repairs on the dunking booth."

"Grandma's been collecting items for the silent auction for at least a month. She's got some really neat things too." Emily shook her head. This wasn't good. "The Smackdown team was planning on doing a demonstration. We've been practicing for weeks." Mrs. Kantola had made them study Rock Harbor history just for the exhibition. "I hope whomever that jacket belongs to goes to see the sheriff."

Caycie stood waiting at the bottom of the bleachers. "Can you believe this?"

Emily hesitated. Why was Caycie being so friendly to her? Emily had volunteered to help with the school's surf team for a few weeks at the start of the school year, but Caycie was a senior, and she hadn't said much to Emily since then. "It's a shock."

"I heard you and your mom were out searching with those dogs. That's pretty cool."

Ah. That explained it. This morning's newscast had not only reported the fire, but had shown Bree and Naomi and Emily in a short video clip about the police working the investigation.

"Yeah." But that's all Emily offered.

Caycie and Trevor moved up in the line at the exit. Ms. Bridges did her best to hand out sheets to the mass of students crowding her.

"Oh, I texted Inetta last night. She's going to meet us at the café after school, so at lunch, call your mom and let her know you're coming home with me after school."

"Did you tell Inetta why you wanted to meet?" Olivia looked a little pale.

"No. I figured we'd tell her together."

Olivia licked her lips. "I'm still a little nervous about telling *anyone*." She glanced around, then lowered her voice even more. "I can't shake the feeling that there's a reason Mom and Dad never told me."

Emily didn't reply. What could she say? Maybe Mr. and Mrs. Webster did have a good reason for keeping Olivia's adoption a secret. But, then again, maybe they didn't.

"I guess there wasn't an e-mail response from Charlotte Tarver, huh?"

Emily shook her head. "Sorry. But maybe today."

The girls took the sheet Ms. Bridges handed them and spilled out of the gym with all the other junior and senior high students.

A slight stench of smoke still lingered in the breezeway, but the school grounds had been picked up since Emily saw it last. Some serious cleaning crews must have worked overtime to get the school ready for classes today.

"Well, we can't exactly contact the attorney offices ourselves."

Emily scanned the sheet. "Oh, look. Yearbook staff has been moved to the school library so the senior high math class can use our classroom."

"At least my morning classes didn't change location." Olivia folded the paper and stuck it in her notebook. "What about yours?"

"Just science, but only moving down three rooms. Guess to make space for the high school science classes."

"Okay. I'll see you at lunch." Olivia shifted her backpack again.

"Yeah. And don't forget to call your mom and tell her you're coming over to my place after school so we can meet Inetta."

"Okay." But Olivia sounded as depressed and upset as she had yesterday and the day before.

Emily gripped her backpack tighter and headed in the opposite direction. It was time she moved into high gear to find out the truth about Olivia's adoption. Her best friend *needed* answers, and Emily was determined to provide them—whether Olivia wanted to hear them or not.

 **SIX**

"Wow. I don't quite know what to say." Inetta stared across the table at Olivia. "How're you doing?"

The Suomi Café wasn't too crowded on the October afternoon. Emily, Olivia, and Inetta had snagged a table in the corner by the window, providing them plenty of privacy for their conversation. Emily had long ago eaten the last bite of her *panukakkua,* a custard pancake drizzled with hot raspberry syrup.

"I don't quite know. I feel like my parents have lied to me all my life, which they have. It hurts."

Inetta reached across the table and squeezed Olivia's hand. "I'm sure they love you to pieces, honey." She flashed a reassuring smile. "There could be a lot of reasons why they didn't tell you."

Olivia nodded.

"We're really hoping that either of the attorneys might be the one referred to on the back of the picture," Emily said. "I haven't gotten a response from Charlotte Tarver's office yet."

"If you do, forward it to me." Inetta jotted down names in her notebook. "I can call first thing in the morning." She tapped her pen against the pad. "Olivia, what's your birth date? And do you know any of the details on your birth certificate, like place of birth, time of birth . . . stuff like that?"

"Did you know that the United States didn't start mandatory registration of births until World War II?" Emily interjected.

Olivia shook her head. "No, but it doesn't surprise me that you do." She rattled off her birth date as Inetta took notes. "I don't know that I've ever actually seen my birth certificate, but I was born on April 18 at Trowbridge Park Hospital, at 7:09 in the evening."

"Really? You know your time of birth off the top of your head?" Inetta asked.

Olivia blushed and smiled. "Mom always told me I was polite, even as a baby, in that I didn't wake her up to be born." Her smile faded. "Of course, now I know that's just another lie."

This time it was Emily who reached over and squeezed her hand. "Don't worry, Liv . . . we're going to find out who your birth parents are."

Olivia frowned.

Inetta's facial expression matched. "Are you sure you don't want to talk with your folks before looking into this? I feel really awkward sticking my nose in here without your parents' permission."

"I'm not sure what I want." Olivia took the last drink of her milk.

"Perhaps you might want to bring up the subject to them and give them the opportunity to tell you the truth." Inetta stirred her coffee absentmindedly.

"They've had fourteen years to tell her, and they haven't." Emily paused as Olivia's head snapped up. Her hands balled into fists as she continued, "I'm sorry to hurt your feelings even more,

Liv, but you know it's true. They've had all this time to tell you, to just say something, but they haven't. Not even when they had the chance."

"What do you mean?" Olivia asked.

"Remember in sixth grade, Mrs. Bridges made us do that family tree? Your mom pulled out all sorts of family history stuff to help you. I remember because I was jealous. Dad didn't keep a lot of stuff when Marika ran off, so I didn't have near the amount of information you had."

"I got an A on the project." Olivia spoke more to herself than to Emily and Inetta. "My documentation was three pages long."

"Right, because you had so much stuff." Emily stared at Inetta. "So her mom had a perfect opening to tell her she was adopted but didn't. I don't think Olivia bringing it up now would make her mom tell her."

"She's right." Olivia set her napkin on top of her plate. "Mom and Dad aren't going to volunteer the information. I'm going to have to find it out myself."

"So why not just tell them you found out?"

Olivia shook her head. "Then I'd have to tell them why I was looking in the chest. I don't want to spoil the surprise of their anniversary party."

Inetta sighed. "Okay, I'll see what I can dig up. I'll text you with anything I find out. In the meantime, if you could find a copy of your birth certificate, that might help." She closed her notebook and shoved it into her purse. She tossed some money on the table by the bill. "I'm sorry to rush off, but I'm hoping to meet up with Sheriff Kaleva when he returns to his office. I want to see if he had any luck."

"I didn't hear that anyone claimed the jacket," Emily said as she and Olivia both stood. "He left the school within an hour of the assembly."

Shoving her purse strap on her shoulder, Inetta led the way out of the café. A sharp breeze kicked up, rustling leaves across the hill. "Oh, no one did. But since the jacket was found in the varsity football locker room, he's going to visit all those players' homes tonight and talk with their parents and show them the jacket."

Emily and Olivia followed her to the sidewalk along Kitchigami Road. Emily shivered. Why hadn't she remembered her jacket this morning? "I wonder if Principal Sturgeon will go through with his threat to cancel the homecoming celebration."

Inetta looked off in the distance, toward Lake Superior.

"What?" Olivia asked.

"I really shouldn't say anything . . ."

"Now you *have* to tell us." Emily pleaded with her eyes, using Timmy's puppy dog eyes and everything.

"Word on the street is that he called all the planners and organizers of the celebration to call it off, but met with so much resistance from the community that he's reconsidering. That's another reason the sheriff's acting so quickly to find out who owns the jacket. It will take some of the pressure off of the principal. He only threatened to call everything off if the jacket's owner wasn't identified." Inetta held up a hand. "But that's not verified yet."

Emily slung her backpack over her shoulder. Actually, he said if no one came forward while the sheriff was at school to claim the jacket . . . but perhaps that was just splitting hairs, as Dad liked to say. "Well, I hope someone can tell him something tonight then."

"Me too," Olivia added.

"Do you girls need a ride home?"

"No, thanks. It's a really short walk." Olivia smiled. "And thanks for checking into things for me."

"I'll text you both when I learn something. Bye." Inetta got into her little Volkswagen Bug, and with a finger wave, hummed off toward Houghton Street.

Emily waved, then turned to Olivia. "I've got to get home. I want to hear what Naomi learned from the vet about Charley. I'm really worried about him."

Olivia nodded. "Call me later. I'll be praying."

"Thanks. I'll be praying for you too." Emily gave Olivia a quick hug and then rushed home.

She ran into the house and then tossed her backpack on the bench in the entry. The enticing scent of stew filled the air. Even though she'd finished her pastry not long ago, her stomach growled at the smell.

"Naomi?"

Sherlock came barreling down the hall and slid on the wood floor. Emily bent and picked him up, snuggling him under her chin.

"In here."

Emily found Naomi and Matthew at the kitchen bar, coloring with markers. The television sitting on the counter was muted but showed the lead-in to the local news segment.

She let Sherlock out the back door, then poured herself a glass of milk. "Where's Timmy?"

"Don't fill up on milk. Dinner's almost ready." Naomi began putting the markers back in the container. "Timmy's over at Dave's. Kade's helping the boys build a clubhouse on stilts, then they're having a club meeting dinner in the backyard."

Emily laughed. "Peanut butter and jelly with crushed-up potato chips, right?"

"So Bree says."

She sat at the table beside Naomi. "What did Dr. Meeks say about Charley?" She took a sip of her milk.

Matthew slammed the coloring book shut and squirmed.

Naomi reached for the rest of the markers. "He doesn't know for sure yet, but he thinks Charley may have ingested something toxic to a dog. He's running tests now and hopes to know something more tomorrow."

"He ate something that made him sick?"

"Apparently."

But Sherlock had gone everywhere Charley had. Even the search last night. Well . . . except for in the beginning when Sherlock didn't follow Samson and Charley, but still.

Emily moved to the window over the kitchen sink and stared into the backyard. Sherlock ran around, chasing dead leaves. "What did he eat that made him so sick?"

"Dr. Meeks said he should know something tomorrow, but for now, he's keeping Charley at the office to monitor him."

Emily glanced out the window at Sherlock again. "Should we take Sherlock in to have tests run?" If anything happened to her puppy . . .

Naomi gave a tired smile as she helped Matthew from the barstool. "No, honey. If Sherlock had ingested something toxic like Charley, he would've showed symptoms even sooner because he's so much younger and smaller."

Thank you, God, for keeping Sherlock safe and for watching over Charley so that he didn't get sicker.

Matthew ran to the back door and hurried outside. Sherlock

met him at the bottom of the stairs, barking and jumping. Naomi put the coloring book and markers in the arts-and-crafts supply cabinet.

"Principal Sturgeon threatened to cancel the homecoming celebration this weekend if no one claimed the jacket we found last night."

"I heard that." Naomi turned up the volume a little on the television, then lifted the lid off the pot and stirred the stew.

The smell made Emily's mouth water. "What do you think about it?" She set her glass on the counter and reached for a stack of bowls from the overhead cabinet.

"I think Principal Sturgeon said what he felt he had to say."

By Naomi's wording, Emily could tell her stepmom didn't think he'd made the right call. She pulled spoons from the drawer. "Nobody claimed the jacket."

Naomi narrowed her eyes. "How do you know that?"

Oh no! She'd done it again: opened her mouth without thinking. And this time, Inetta *had* said the information wasn't verified, which was definitely code for "don't tell anyone."

"Emily?"

She swallowed and set the spoons on the counter beside the bowls. "Sheriff Kaleva left the school too quickly. If someone had come forward, he would've called their parents and had them come to the school, right?"

Naomi crossed her arms over her chest. "Em-i-ly."

She let out a heavy sigh and told her stepmom what Inetta had said. "But that's not verified or anything yet." She avoided eye contact with Naomi, staring instead at the television.

Was that Sheriff Kaleva?

"Emily, how many times have we—"

"Look. At the TV." She turned up the volume.

On the screen, Sheriff Kaleva, holding the clear plastic bag containing the fleece jacket, appeared larger than in person. "We're asking for all the residents of Rock Harbor to help out." He raised the bag higher, and the camera zoomed in on the jacket. "If you recognize this jacket or know who it belongs to, please contact the Rock Harbor Sheriff's Office immediately. Thank you."

The screen panned back to the five o'clock anchorman. "Thank you, Sheriff Mason Kaleva." He stared directly into the camera. "The number for the sheriff's office is there at the bottom of your screen. If you have any information regarding the jacket Sheriff Kaleva just showed you, please call the number at the bottom of your screen now."

"In other news . . ." The coanchor launched into a report on storm safety tips.

Emily turned down the volume again. "Looks like the information was verified after all."

"That's not exactly the point," Naomi said.

Brrrrring!

"I'll get it." Emily rushed to grab the phone. "Hello?"

Nothing.

"Hello?"

Emily started to hang up, but then heard breathing. Very faint. She checked the caller ID: *unknown*.

"Who is this?"

"Em—" Then the phone went dead.

The room shifted, like in an earthquake. Emily's heart pounded so hard she thought her ribs might crack. She gripped the cordless phone tight and leaned against the kitchen bar. The corner dug into her side.

Breathing no longer came naturally. She had to force the air in and out of her lungs.

"Emily?" Naomi glanced up and caught sight of Emily's face. She set down the serving spoon and rushed to Emily's side. She pried the phone from Emily's hand. "Hello?"

She turned the phone off and set it on the counter. "Emily, you're white as a sheet. Who was that?"

"I—I—I think it was Marika." Again. Why couldn't she leave her alone?

The wind whistled through the trees, and moonlight bounced off the whitecaps. Emily zipped her coat as high as it would go and snapped her hood under her chin. "We'll never find the dog out here. How can Samson smell it out over the water?" She did *not* want to get in that boat, but Bree stood with her hand out and she had no choice.

Bree helped Emily aboard the motorboat. "The moisture enhances the odor for the dogs."

The call had come right after a gloomy dinner. A family had been getting their boat docked for the winter, and their beloved dog had leaped overboard. Emily had been glad to get out of the house and quit worrying that her mother would call back. But a water search was not high on her list of things she wanted to experience—especially at night.

Her pulse throbbed in her throat. "Are you sure you need me?"

Bree patted the seat beside her. "This is part of your training. And with Charley sick, it will help to have Sherlock along for a second nose—it's good training for him too. The dog has been in the water for an hour, so I'm not hopeful, but we have to try."

Naomi handed her a life jacket. "Put this on. Are you warm enough?"

"Not really. Maybe I should wait in the car. The wind is really cold." Maybe Naomi would take pity and let her stay behind.

Naomi dug in her pocket. "Here, take my gloves. And sit behind the windshield."

"I've got gloves." Emily pulled them from her pocket. "I've got homework to do too."

Naomi frowned. "It's not like you to want to sit out on a search. Are you getting sick?"

Emily had worked hard to overcome her fear of the water over the years, and she wasn't about to admit her knees were shaking. "I'm just cold." She moved to the seat Naomi pointed out.

"I've got the dog's blanket." Bree held the fluffy blue scrap of material under Samson's nose. He sniffed it eagerly.

Emily got back up and led her puppy to the blanket. "Smell that, Sherlock." The puppy sniffed around the material, but he was more interested in Samson.

"Search, Samson," Bree commanded.

The dog whined and moved to the front of the boat with his nose into the wind. Emily eyed him doubtfully. His tail wagged and his ears were at attention. Sherlock followed him, but he was more interested in the boat than the scent.

"How will you even know if he smells something?"

"By his manner," Bree explained. "He'll bark or lean forward more. Samson sometimes even climbs out on the bow of the boat."

Bree started the engine, and the boat pulled away from the harbor. The bow of the boat slammed into the choppy waves, and Emily steadied herself on the side. Nausea made her swallow several times. All she wanted was for this trip to be over and for her feet to be back on solid ground.

"The dog went into the water about here, as near as I can tell," Bree said, slowing the boat. The boat bobbed in the waves as she killed the engine. "Give the dogs a refresher sniff."

Emily didn't want to let go of the side of the boat, but she grabbed the blanket and eased up to where Samson and Sherlock could smell it. Samson took another whiff and then whined eagerly. He jumped onto the bow of the boat and went out to the very front.

"He's going to fall in!" Emily tried to reach Samson's leash and failed, but she did grab Sherlock's. Sherlock wanted to follow, but Emily held his leash tight. Her puppy wasn't as experienced as Samson, and she didn't want him to tumble into the icy water.

"Samson is very sure-footed," Bree said. "I think he smells something. What is it, boy? Where is Jasper?"

Samson barked. His tail swished wildly. He crouched on the tip of the boat until his feet hung over. Emily strained to see in the dark, but she couldn't see anything in the choppy water.

"There!" Naomi pointed. "What's that? It looks like a flotation cushion. And I think that's the Vesterses' boat."

"Mrs. Vesters told me she threw one in hoping Jasper could get to it." Bree started the engine again and cruised near the other boat. When they reached the Vesterses' boat, she cut the engine again.

Mrs. Vesters grabbed the rope Bree threw her. "He hasn't barked in ages." Her long blond hair was pulled back in a pony-tail, and her cheeks were red from the cold wind.

"I thought I saw a flotation cushion," Naomi said.

Mr. Vesters nodded. He worked in the shipyard and was a big

bear of a man in his twenties with a black mustache. "We threw it as close as we could, but Jasper never made it onto the cushion."

Emily wanted to cry. The poor little dog probably drowned. Her hold on the side of the boat eased, and she concentrated on trying to see some small speck in the water. The dogs were still acting as though they smelled something. Samson hadn't left his perch on the bow. His nose pointed north, and he whined.

"Let's try that direction," Emily said, pointing. "I think Samson smells something."

Bree nodded and pulled in her rope, then started the engine again. They motored toward the northern cliff face. Emily forgot about the cold and the scary waves. Where was Jasper? Samson whined and barked. His nails scraped on the boat as he tried to wiggle closer to the water.

Emily glanced at Bree. "Is he reacting?"

Bree nodded. "And he's not giving a death reaction. I think Jasper is still alive."

Emily straightened and called to the little dog, "Jasper!" She leaned over the side of the boat by a few inches. Where was he? He was white and tan, so he wasn't going to be easy to spot in the whitecaps.

Sherlock barked too, his paws up on the side of the boat. He seemed to be staring at something in the water, but Emily couldn't see what. She shouted for Jasper again and listened. Was that a weak whine? Squinting, she looked as hard as she could. A small curl of a wave parted to reveal a dog in the cold water. He was lying on a scrap of wood.

Thank you, God! Emily leaped to her feet and pointed. "There he is! Hey, Jasper, hey, boy. We're going to get you out of there." She looked at Bree, who seemed grim. "We are, aren't we?"

"I'm afraid the wake of our boat is going to knock him into the water. You ready to go get him, Naomi?"

Naomi reached for her backpack. "Sure am. Let me get on my dry suit and fins."

The thought of Naomi in that high surf made Emily's mouth go dry. "Can't we snag him with an oar or something?"

Bree shook her head. "We sit up too high in the water."

Emily hadn't thought through how they were going to rescue the little dog. She moved nearer to Naomi. "How can I help?"

"When I'm in the water, it will be harder to see where he is. You'll need to direct me." Naomi zipped up her suit, then reached into the pack and pulled out some blankets. "Wait by the ladder with blankets for both of us. We'll need them."

Emily clutched the blankets to her chest and nodded. Naomi snapped on her fins, then jumped into the water. The cold spray struck Emily in the face, and she winced. The water in Superior was always cold, but this time of year it was nearly freezing. Naomi could get hypothermia pretty quickly out there.

She stood and pointed. "There he is, Naomi. About ten feet to your right at about two o'clock."

Naomi waved a hand, then struck out in Jasper's direction. In moments she reached the dog. Clutching him to her chest, she side paddled slowly, with his muzzle on her shoulder out of the water, until she was nearly to the boat.

Emily eased herself down on the ladder by one rung, only a foot above the water. "Hand him up to me."

Naomi lifted the drenched and shivering dog up to her. "Hang on tight."

"Got him." Emily clutched Jasper to her chest and climbed back to the deck, where she wrapped the blanket around him.

She turned and handed the other blanket to Naomi as she came up the ladder. "Your lips are blue."

"That water is freezing!" Naomi wrapped herself in the blanket, then pulled out another blanket and wrapped herself in it too. "Let's get him to the vet."

"I just called his owners and told them to meet us there. They're already on their way to the dock." Bree started the motor.

Emily unzipped her coat and put the shivering dog inside. She'd been only a *little* afraid.

 **SEVEN**

"I can't believe Principal Sturgeon hasn't had an assembly all day." Emily shoved books into her locker, then slammed the door shut. She didn't even need a notebook for yearbook staff class. "It's clear no one claimed the jacket because the sheriff was on the news last night asking for the owner to come forward."

Olivia shrugged. "Maybe someone came forward after the news last night. Or this morning." She had yearbook with Emily, so she fell into step alongside her.

"I don't think so."

"Why not?"

Emily nodded at the front circle of the school. The sheriff's car sat parked right out front. "I don't think he'd be here if they'd found the owner of the jacket. They'd have them down at the station, not here at the school."

"You never know." Olivia led the way into the media center. "I miss our classroom already. It's hard to work on layouts and designs without all our stuff."

"Yeah, me too." Emily sat at one of the round tables, Olivia taking the chair beside her. As they waited for class to start, she told Olivia about her adventure on the lake.

"Wow, *you* went out in a boat? And climbed down the ladder? I'm impressed."

"I'm a little impressed with myself too." Emily grinned and took out a book. "It was less scary once I was focused on that poor dog. I'm actually kinda excited to try another water rescue."

Mr. Morris, the yearbook sponsor, entered the media center. The few hairs left on the top of his head stood up from the wind. The media center was located on the main breezeway, and it was almost always windy. Today the hint of smoke still lingered on the east end of the school.

"Students, most of our needed tools will be brought to the media center tomorrow, so for today, I'd like you to review previous issues of the yearbook to see which layouts you think worked best." Mr. Morris smoothed his hair. "Upon approval, you and your team will be allowed to recreate that layout in the current yearbook." He gestured to the various yearbooks lying on the main table. "Begin."

"I'll get one." Olivia jumped up from her seat and rushed to the main table, apparently determined to get first pick.

Emily stared out the window into the parking lot. She caught herself automatically searching for Marika. Naomi had called the sheriff after Marika's call last night, but he said there wasn't really anything they could do. He suggested they change their number to an unlisted one, but Dad and Naomi talked about it and decided not to, since it was too easy to get anyone's phone number in Rock Harbor. They did decide to upgrade the phone service and have auto-reject on any unknown or private number.

"What are you staring at?" Olivia nudged Emily.

"Oh, nothing." Emily smiled. "Was just daydreaming." She hadn't told Olivia about Marika's call. She didn't like talking about Marika. Besides, as Sheriff Kaleva pointed out, there was no way to know for certain the caller had really been Marika.

Except Emily knew it was. She was absolutely certain.

Olivia snorted and sat down, setting last year's annual in front of Emily. She opened the book. "Well, stop daydreaming and start focusing. I want to find a really good layout for the Fashion Club's page."

Emily grinned back and opened the yearbook. "Got it."

"Hey"—Olivia stopped flipping pages—"when do you think you'll get back to making your jewelry?"

As much as Emily loved making beaded necklaces, bracelets, and earrings, she loved SAR more. "Maybe once Sherlock's trained. Between training and Smackdown practices and studying, I just don't have the time." She turned to the back of the yearbook, where most of the freestyle layouts were. "Speaking of time . . . are you working on your parents' anniversary party? Naomi ordered the cake for you with their wedding picture."

Olivia nodded. "I turned the invitations over to Mrs. Heinonen to address and mail. Your grandma is the best."

Actually, Martha Heinonen was Naomi's mother, but she loved Emily and Timmy just as much as she loved Matthew. She could be a little stuffy and formal sometimes, but Emily adored her.

"It's hard working on the party." Olivia's nose scrunched. "I mean, they're my parents and I love them and want to celebrate their anniversary, but . . . well . . ."

"It's hard to do something for them when they've kept the secret that you're adopted all these years."

"Does that make me a selfish person?"

"Of course not. Don't be silly. You're one of the most generous people I know." Emily couldn't think of many people more giving than Olivia. "Have you had any luck finding your birth certificate?"

"Not yet. Mom and Dad have their monthly meeting with Pastor Lukkari tonight, so I'm hoping to have a chance to look in the trunk again."

"Do you want me to come help?"

"No. I need to do it alone."

"I understand." And she did, but she still really wanted to help her friend.

Olivia didn't reply; she just turned the page.

Wanting to give Olivia the moment she obviously needed, Emily focused on the pages in the yearbook in front of her. She could only imagine how Olivia felt. If it'd been her, Emily would've already confronted her parents. The curiosity to know would have outweighed anything else.

She flipped to the next page, barely glancing at the photographs or the layout. After school tonight, she had to study for the *Smackdown* exhibition or she'd embarrass herself and the team at the homecoming demonstration. If Principal Sturgeon didn't have it canceled. Then again, if the community demanded the celebration happen regardless, like Inetta had heard . . .

"Did Naomi call Dr. Meeks this morning?" Olivia asked, interrupting Emily's thoughts.

"He said Charley was about the same as before, but tests should be back today." Naomi had tried to hide how worried she was, but Emily understood. They all loved Charley and missed him. If something happened to Sherlock, Emily would be a total wreck.

"I'm still praying."

"Thanks." Emily was too. A lot. For Charley. For Naomi. For Olivia and her parents. She turned to the next page in the yearbook.

And froze. Her heart kicked up a notch as she let out a little gasp.

"What?" Olivia leaned over and stared at the picture on the page.

In front of the football field, several juniors hammed it up for the camera by striking "bodybuilder" poses.

"Do you see it?" Emily whispered.

Olivia shook her head. "What? It's just a bunch of guys goofing off. Nothing special about the layout."

Emily tapped her finger on one of the boys in the picture.

"Drake Wilson?"

"Look at what he's wearing," Emily whispered.

"Oh."

It was the blue fleece jacket.

Olivia licked her lips. "Maybe it's not the same kind or same shade of blue."

Emily arched a single brow, a talent she had only recently perfected. "I was there when it was found, remember? It's the same color and style. It has that little logo on the sleeve too, see? And Drake's on the varsity football team, so he has access to the locker room."

"But Drake?"

Emily understood. Drake was the son of the county coroner and a local hairdresser. He was an honor student, running back for the varsity football team, and one of the nicest seniors in the whole school. He'd even been voted junior favorite last year.

"I could be wrong, I guess." It didn't make any sense. Why would Drake have had anything to do with a fire?

Olivia leaned closer as other kids moved to the table beside her and Emily. "You have to tell Principal Sturgeon."

"I can't." But Emily's heartbeat quickened.

"You have to, Em."

"What will the whole school think? They'll label me a snitch. That'd be social suicide for sure, Liv."

"It's not just the school. The police are involved. You don't have a choice." Olivia grabbed the yearbook and handed it to Emily. "You have to take this to the office and tell Principal Sturgeon."

Emily twirled her hair around her finger. What was she supposed to do? If she told on Drake, she'd never be popular, and she would go into high school next year with everyone hating her.

"Emily."

"I'm not sure. I mean, like you said, it could very well not be the same jacket."

"But it could be."

It could be the kiss of death on her high school social life. "Remember Inetta said Sheriff Kaleva was visiting all the varsity players' homes last night. He probably already talked with Drake and his parents."

"Emily, quit making excuses." Olivia always called Emily out—but in a good way.

"I just don't see the point in getting Drake in trouble when I really don't *know* it's the same jacket, you know?"

Olivia shook her head. "Just a second ago, you were pretty sure it was." She pointed a finger, right at Emily's face. "You aren't thinking about Drake . . . you're thinking about how people will talk about you for saying anything."

Heat shot up the back of Emily's neck and spread across her

face. She knew going to the principal was the right thing to do, but she also knew what it could cost her. Just this past Sunday, Pastor Lukkari had led the discussion around Deuteronomy 6:18 about doing what is right. Period. No discussion.

Emily stood.

"Em?"

She lifted the yearbook. "I'm telling Mr. Morris I need to see Principal Sturgeon."

Ten minutes later, she sat on the row of chairs outside the principal's office. She clutched the yearbook, her finger inserted to keep the place of the photograph. Teachers and kids alike stared at her as they passed in the hall, the area usually reserved for those in trouble. She would almost rather be in trouble than be labeled a snitch.

Do what is right and good in the LORD's sight, so that it may go well with you . . .

Yeah, telling the principal was the right thing to do, but that didn't mean she had to like it. Not when it meant she'd be the social outcast of Rock Harbor School, which would probably lead into being a town outcast.

"Emily." Principal Sturgeon opened his door and waved her into his office.

She dragged her feet as she followed him inside, then took a seat in one of the two chairs facing his desk.

Principal Sturgeon was almost as tall as Dad, but with a lot more gray hair and didn't look like he ate as healthy as Naomi made Dad eat. He plopped down into his chair. It made a couple of popping sounds. "Now, what can I do for you, Ms. O'Reilly?"

"It's about the jacket." Forcing the words past the lump in her throat was harder than she'd thought.

"Yes?"

She flipped open the yearbook to the page with the picture. She set it on his desk in front of him and pointed at the picture. Maybe if she didn't say anything, just showed him the picture and let him figure it out, she wouldn't actually be snitching. Not really.

"What does this photo have to do with the jac—" His eyes widened. "I see. Thank you for bringing this to my attention, Ms. O'Reilly."

She stood, clasping her hands in front of her. "Can I go now?"

"You may."

"Um, Principal Sturgeon . . ."

"Yes?"

"I'd really prefer not to have it announced that I'm the one who brought this to your attention." It sounded so shallow when she said it. *God, I'm doing what I know is right. I just don't want to have everybody hate me because I did.*

"I understand."

She left his office with her head ducked. Three high school boys sat in the row of chairs outside the principal's office. Their stares followed her as she moved down the hall.

"I'll be with you boys in just a moment." Principal Sturgeon's voice boomed throughout the office. "Ms. Givens, can you get Sheriff Kaleva on the phone, please? And get me Drake Wilson's home address."

Emily's heart dropped to her stomach as she pushed open the office door and stepped into the breezeway. So much for remaining anonymous.

Her popularity points would be in the negatives by this time tomorrow. Great. Just great.

 **EIGHT**

"Pyrethrin?" Emily stared at Naomi over the kitchen table, tuning out Sherlock's whining at the back door.

"Dr. Meeks said all the tests were conclusive. Charley definitely ingested pyrethrin." Her stepmom frowned as she dabbed her mouth with a napkin. "It's a chemical found in insect sprays. You can buy them over the counter."

"But we don't have any insect sprays here because of Matthew, right?" She looked at her father.

Dad shook his head. "No, we don't."

"Is Charley gonna be okay?" Timmy took another bite of the borscht.

"Don't talk with your mouth full," Naomi corrected him. "Dr. Meeks said Charley should be fine after his treatment. Matter of fact, if he does well on his treatment plan, Dr. Meeks said he'd bring him home this weekend."

"Good." Timmy slurped milk from his glass as Matthew reached for the salt.

Naomi moved the saltshaker out of Matthew's reach. Matthew turned in his seat to stick his tongue out at Timmy.

Emily forced a sip of water down. "What kind of treatment?" At least they knew what it was, and at least it was treatable. She couldn't imagine how she'd feel if . . . well, she wouldn't even think like that. *Thank you, God, for letting Charley get treatment to make him better.*

"Well, right now they're giving Charley medication to control the muscle tremors, which is what Timmy saw. They have him on an IV so he doesn't get dehydrated and he can get his medication to counteract the poison directly into his bloodstream."

The word *poison* slammed against Emily's brain. "How did Charley eat poison that we don't have around here?" She listened carefully to make sure she could still hear Sherlock at the back door. Maybe his whining wasn't such a nuisance after all.

Naomi's frowned deepened. "We don't know for sure. Maybe when he was at the school after the fire. It's possible some of the toxin was spilled."

Toxin. Another word that rubbed wrong against Emily. Sherlock had been at the school, and he wasn't nearly as smart as Charley. "The school science lab had this stuff?"

"No."

Good thing. Emily could think of some of the older kids who weren't as careful as they should be. It was bad enough when nontoxic stuff got spilled. "Is it used to put out fires?"

Naomi swallowed and looked at Dad, who took a sip of his water and set the glass down. "No. Not according to the fire chief."

"So why would it be spilled at the fire scene?" Surely they

wouldn't use anything toxic or poisonous at the school science lab. Not like that. "Is it flammable?"

"For the most part, no." Dad held his fork midair. "And before you ask, no one has any idea why it would be at the school."

Sherlock whined. Her stare stuck on the back door.

"According to Dr. Meeks, symptoms appear within six hours. Sherlock's fine." Naomi smiled. "But go ahead and let him in. I know it will make you feel better."

Emily jumped from her seat and flung the back door open. Sherlock skidded on the wood floor. Matthew clapped.

Naomi turned and snapped, then pointed. "Sit." Sherlock dropped to his haunches. "Stay." Her voice was firm, just like Bree taught everyone at the school.

Emily ate a bite of soup, her mind still processing. "So we really don't know how he got the stuff, right? It could've been at the school, but it could've been somewhere else. Right?" Charley got the poison somewhere Sherlock wasn't, because if Charley drank something while Sherlock was around, Sherlock would've gotten sick too. If what Dr. Meeks said was true about the six hours, then Charley would've had to drink it Tuesday night to have symptoms on Wednesday morning.

But Sherlock was with Charley all of Tuesday, even at night. How did Charley drink the poison and not Sherlock?

Unless someone *gave* the poison to Charley.

Emily's stomach tightened, and she set her spoon atop her saucer, ignoring the uneaten slice of Ruis bread sitting there. "Could someone have poisoned Charley on purpose?"

Matthew and Timmy ceased their discussion on airplanes. "Someone poisoned Charley?" Timmy asked.

"We don't know that," Naomi replied.

"It's the only thing that makes sense." Emily turned away from Dad's scowl. She didn't want to upset Timmy, or Matthew either, but Timmy wasn't a baby and he loved Charley.

Naomi pressed her lips together.

"We've requested Dr. Meeks give Sheriff Kaleva all the information. If Mason finds anything suspicious, he'll open a full investigation. Until then, we won't assume." Dad's voice left no room for argument.

She ducked her head and drank the last of her water, but she wasn't buying the *no assumption* bit. Emily could tell by Naomi's lips forming a straight line that she couldn't explain how Charley had gotten the poison. By the sternness of her expression, it was clear she wasn't happy about not having the answer.

Neither was Emily. It could easily be Sherlock at the vet hospital, and as a small puppy, he would have been in a lot more danger than Charley had been.

There was just so much going on: the fire . . . Charley being poisoned . . . Olivia's adoption . . . Marika calling.

Emily started to ask another question, then caught the way Dad and Naomi were looking at each other. They were dealing with a lot too. Maybe it was better to just wait until they heard what Sheriff Kaleva thought.

"I'm sorry for calling so late." Inetta sounded concerned. "But I needed to talk to you."

Emily glanced at the clock on her computer. It was only seven. What did Inetta think: she was ten? "It's fine. What's up?" She moved to sit on the floor and pet Sherlock's ears. They were so soft and silky. She loved the feel of them.

"Did you receive a response from Charlotte Tarver's office?"

"No. Have you found out anything?" Emily rolled Sherlock onto his back, rubbing the side of his belly until his leg moved in automatic response.

"Kinda. I had a friend of mine, an investigator, call. He told me the private investigator that freelances for the Tarver Agency had done a little research on me."

"Why?"

"Well, that's what I don't know for sure." Inetta's voice still sounded pretty strained. "We're working on getting answers, but the only thing I can think that would prompt attention is the queries I put out about Charlotte Tarver."

Sherlock licked Emily's chin. "I don't understand."

"For a private investigator to be poking around about me, I've hit a nerve somewhere. In my experience, that usually means someone is checking me out because I've been checking them out and it's made them nervous."

"Like they have something to hide?" Was there something to Olivia's adoption like she'd thought? Maybe her birth parents really *were* in witness protection or something.

"I don't know. I think maybe I should tell your parents what's going on."

Oh no. Dad would be angry that she'd been nosing around in something that was none of her business. And Naomi? Well, she'd be hurt that Emily hadn't told her. But she'd promised Olivia she wouldn't say anything. "Why? There's no point. I haven't even gotten a response, and I remembered to check my spam and junk mail folders."

"Then maybe I'm wrong. But just in case, don't do any more searches on Charlotte Tarver. At least until I can find out what's what."

Emily got off the floor and sat on the edge of her bed. "Should I do anything else instead? Like see if I can find anything more at Olivia's house? She's looking for a copy of her birth certificate tonight."

"That's fine, but it probably won't yield any new information. Just don't do any more research right now until I know for sure." Inetta coughed. "Hey, on a different subject, do you know Drake Wilson?"

Her heartbeat sped up a notch at just the mention of his name. Lodging the cell between her shoulder and her cheek, Emily grabbed her UGG slipper just before Sherlock bit it. "I know who he is, but I don't know him, know him. Why?"

"Sheriff Kaleva is on his way to his house to take him and his parents to the sheriff's office for questioning. It seems he's the owner of the jacket found at the scene."

Her mouth went dry. "The sheriff isn't going to talk to him and his parents at their house?"

"He lied to the sheriff last night when he was asked about the jacket."

Emily tossed the chew toy on the ground for Sherlock. "So he's in trouble?"

"He is. His father, as county coroner, is going to be really upset. It's a big mess. I'm waiting for the sheriff's office to make an official statement."

This wasn't good. "Even if that jacket is Drake's, that doesn't mean he was involved in the fire."

"I don't know, Em. His not coming forward when he had the

chance is really suspicious. At least, that's what I hear from my sources."

Emily didn't know what to say. Then again, she'd probably said too much anyway already. She felt nervous butterflies in her stomach.

"I have to run. I just wanted to check in with you about Charlotte Tarver."

"Okay. Thanks. Let me know if you learn anything else."

"I will. Oh, and Em?"

"Yeah?"

"Please don't say anything about Drake being questioned. I need to get the sheriff's statement first."

"Sure." The one word caught in her throat as she disconnected the call and then set the cell on her desk.

Her hands shook a little, and her first instinct was to call Olivia. But what if Mrs. Webster answered? Emily didn't know what to say, exactly. Sure, she could tell Olivia about Drake being taken in, but she couldn't—no, wouldn't—say anything about Charlotte Tarver.

The doorbell rang.

Maybe there was news about Charley's poisoning. She could hear Naomi reading Matthew a bedtime story as she headed down the hall, Sherlock growling as he followed her.

When she got to the door, she found Dad and Sheriff Kaleva walking into the living room.

Emily snapped and pointed at Sherlock. "Sit. Stay." She made sure to keep her voice firm. Bree would be proud.

The sheriff held his hat in his hands. "I'm sorry to bother you, Donovan, but I don't want Bree out near the woods alone."

"What's going on?" Naomi entered the living room and took Dad's hand.

"Missing boy. We're pretty sure he's run away." Sheriff Kaleva stared hard at Emily.

Who was missing?

"How can I help?" Naomi asked. "Charley's still at the vet's."

Sheriff Kaleva nodded. "I know, but I really don't feel good about Bree doing a search by herself in the woods."

Naomi had already moved to the hall closet and snagged her jacket. "I'll meet her there."

Emily moved to the closet as well. "We can take Sherlock. He might be able to help."

Sherlock's body shivered at the mention of his name, but he didn't move from his spot. It was as if he knew he was being tested.

Naomi hesitated for just a moment before looking at Emily's father. "It'd be an extra nose in the woods." She held the ready pack in her hand.

Dad paused. Emily's muscles tightened. "Please, Dad. Let me help Bree and Naomi. And the missing boy. I know how scary being in the woods at night can be."

He let out a sigh and nodded.

"Bree said she was heading to the Kitchigami Wilderness Preserve, near Pakkala Road." The sheriff plopped his hat back onto his head.

"Who's missing?" Emily reached for Sherlock's vest on the hanger, then slipped it over his wagging body.

"Drake Wilson."

 **NINE**

They got out of the SUV behind Drake's red Neon. A cold wind blew out of the north, snaking icy fingers down Emily's coat. "Why hasn't Samson found a scent?" She yanked gloves from her pocket and pulled them on.

Bree stopped and cracked open a pistachio. "We might have started in the wrong place. The sheriff didn't know where he might have gone."

The dogs nosed along a fence, but they clearly had no scent. The moon was out, but it cast little light over the dark landscape.

Emily stuffed her hands in her pockets. "Why didn't we start at his house?"

Naomi shrugged. "He took his car, and the dogs can't track him when he's in an enclosed space. His car was parked along the road here, so it made sense to give it a try."

"What if he got in another car here?"

Bree gasped. "Good idea, Emily. Maybe a friend met him. Does he have a girlfriend?"

She thought about it. "Not that I know of. He mostly hangs out with the school jocks. I haven't seen him talking to anyone special at school."

She watched Samson's tail go up. "Hey, I think he's got something!"

Bree beat her to the dog's side. He was dancing around a spot on the ground. "What you got there, boy?" She knelt on the frosted grass and peered around. "Hand me some gloves, Naomi." When Naomi handed her some, Bree pulled them on and felt through the weeds. "He's smelling something." She flipped her flashlight on, and the beam pushed back the edges of darkness.

Careful not to touch anything, Emily knelt beside her. "I don't see anything." By now Sherlock had joined Samson. Tail wagging, the puppy seemed oblivious to the scent.

"Ah, what's this?" Bree picked up something and held it under the light. "It's a ski hat."

Samson barked happily and ran in circles. "This must be Drake's, from the way Samson is acting."

Emily stood and dusted her hands off on her jeans. "But it's not cold enough for a ski hat. I mean, yeah, it's chilly, but this is for serious cold."

"Maybe it fell out of his pocket," Naomi suggested.

"The dogs should be able to lead us from here if he dropped it," Bree said. She dropped the hat into a bag and held it under Samson's nose. "Search, boy!"

"Let Sherlock try," Naomi said. Emily shot her a smile, and she smiled back. "He's itching to get involved."

And the puppy *did* seem eager. He plunged his nose into the bag, then followed Samson around the open field as if he knew what he was doing.

Bree watched the dogs with a frown that deepened in moments. "They aren't getting a scent."

"How can that be?" Emily asked. "He was right here. He didn't just disappear."

"I think that's it. He wasn't here at all. Maybe someone else had his hat and dropped it out here."

Naomi was frowning too. "But his car is here."

"True enough. Let's go back there."

They retraced their steps to the Neon. When Bree opened the door, Samson thrust his head inside and barked. Sherlock yipped and wagged his tail. Bree put her hand on his head. "It's definitely Drake's car."

"Maybe the car broke down, and he called someone to come get him," Emily suggested. This was very weird, and her stomach clenched.

"Maybe. The sheriff is checking out his friends," Bree said.

"What if we drive up and down the road with the windows down? The dogs might catch something," Emily said.

Bree and Naomi exchanged a long glance, then Bree shrugged. "It's worth a try."

At least they weren't treating her like a kid. They piled back into the SUV and ran the windows down. Both dogs hung their heads out. Emily fastened her seat belt, and Bree drove down the road slowly. Several times they stopped, thinking the dogs had a scent, but each time failed to trigger an alert. The clock on the dash glowed nearly eleven when they got back in the car the last time.

"We might as well give this up for tonight," Bree said. "Maybe the sheriff is having better luck finding him."

Emily bit her lip. She'd thought the dogs could *always* find a missing person.

"I already got your books for you." Olivia leaned against Emily's locker. "Aren't you glad it's Friday? Come on, let's go to homeroom."

Something was up. "We have almost ten minutes until first bell rings." She yawned. It'd been after eleven by the time she and Naomi got home, and another couple of hours before she'd been able to fall asleep. She hadn't been able to stop thinking about Drake. She couldn't believe the dogs couldn't find him. And she felt like it was all her fault that he was missing and alone. "Hey, did you find a copy of your birth certificate last night?"

"No. Come on, let's walk to class."

"Okay, 'cause I have something to tell you. I just need to hang my jacket in my locker." Emily held up her Windbreaker. She didn't think she could face all day at school, but if she hadn't come, no way would Dad or Naomi let her go on any more night searches. "Move and let me stick it in my locker, then we can go talk and you can tell me what's going on."

When Naomi called the sheriff that morning for an update on Drake and was told he still hadn't been found, Emily had felt like she was going to be sick. She felt so guilty about turning that picture in. What if Drake had run away because he was innocent and someone else was framing him? Or because the fire was a horrible accident? And now he was alone in the woods, hungry and scared and maybe hurt—and it was all her fault. She needed to talk it out, and the only person she wanted to do that with was Liv.

Olivia didn't move.

Emily shifted her weight from one leg to the other. What was wrong with Olivia?

"Liv?"

Just then, several high school kids walked by.

"Snitch," someone said in a cough-like bark.

One of them bumped her, knocking her into Olivia, then they all laughed before moving on down the hall.

Heat flooded her face as her heart slammed against her ribs.

"I'm so sorry, Em," Olivia whispered as she bent to pick up the lunch bag Emily had dropped.

Emily caught sight of her locker over Olivia's shoulder. Someone had written in a black marker across the front, EMILY O'REILLY IS A SNITCH.

Tears burned her eyes. She blinked hard and fast. She. Would. Not. Let. Them. See. Her. Cry.

Lord, why? I did the right thing, right? So how come no one understands that?

Olivia put her arm around Emily's shoulder and led her toward homeroom. "Ignore them. They're just being bullies."

A funny taste filled Emily's mouth. "I told you this would happen if I went to Principal Sturgeon." Her social life, or whatever one she'd ever dreamed of having, was over. Before it ever really started.

"This will all blow over in a few days, especially once everyone has a great time at the homecoming celebration, which we wouldn't even be having if it weren't for you." Olivia led her down the hall. "You did the right thing."

Right thing—maybe. Social suicide—definitely.

"Emily. Emily," called out someone from behind them.

She stopped and turned, facing Rachel Zinn.

"Oh my gosh, are you okay? I heard from some of the high schoolers you told on Drake—that it was his jacket the sheriff found, and that's why he ran away."

Emily and Rachel had been friends in elementary grades, then had a rough patch during the beginning of middle school. They'd recently ironed out their differences, but Rachel wasn't exactly a comforting type of friend.

"Drake probably ran away because he lied to the sheriff." Olivia, ever the defender, stood beside Emily like Sherlock over his favorite toy. "Emily didn't get Drake in trouble. Drake got himself in trouble."

"Hey, I'm not accusing. I'm just saying what I heard." Rachel ignored Olivia, staring at Emily.

Emily needed to know. "Who said I told on Drake?"

Rachel shrugged. "A couple of high school boys saw you leave the principal's office, then heard Principal Sturgeon ask for the sheriff and Drake's address. They called Drake and warned him."

That made sense. Emily licked her lips. "I saw a picture of Drake wearing the jacket we found at the school the night of the fire. I told the principal so he could look into it because it was possible Drake had given the jacket to someone else, his mom could've donated it for the yard sale, or maybe he'd loaned it to a friend, anything like that. I didn't say Drake set the fire. I just told him so that he could talk to Drake and maybe come closer to finding who did it so we wouldn't lose homecoming." If only she could take it back, she would.

Rachel nodded. "That makes sense. My dad's always giving away stuff he doesn't use. And some stuff I still want."

The first bell rang.

"See you around, Rachel. And thanks for letting us know what everyone is saying." Olivia was still in protective mode as she turned Emily toward their homeroom. "Ignore everyone, Em. Seriously."

Just outside the classroom door, Olivia pulled her to the side. "Listen, I found something in the trunk last night."

Her dying social life momentarily forgotten, Emily widened her eyes. "Your birth certificate?"

Olivia shook her head. "Maybe better. I found an old envelope that had a document from the Michigan Department of Health. It lists my birth mother's name."

Excitement rushed through Emily. "Well?"

Olivia's expression was unreadable. "My birth mother was Mackenzie Barnes."

Mackenzie Barnes. Emily had never heard the name before.

"I don't know who that is, but I texted the information to Inetta."

The second bell rang, ending the conversation. They joined the other students filing into English class. But at least now they had a name. It was a start.

They'd barely taken their seats when the morning announcements started. "Students, I'm pleased to inform you that since the jacket's owner has been identified by a fellow student, the homecoming celebration tomorrow at the community center is back on." Principal Sturgeon's voice boomed over the intercom. "I hope to see everyone at the football game tonight. Don't forget, it begins at seven."

The intercom squealed before it shut off, then everyone was silent. Seconds slipped by, then a couple of kids turned to stare at Emily.

"What're you staring at?" Olivia asked one of the football players who glared at Emily.

"We'll probably lose the game tonight since our starting running back is missing because of you."

A couple of other kids nodded, and a lot of people were looking at her and whispering. Emily wanted to run away herself. To the bathroom to throw up. To go back to bed and pull the covers over her head. She had thought everyone would be excited that the celebration was back on, but instead it seemed to make them hate her more. Why couldn't this all be a horribly bad dream?

Her life had become a nightmare.

TEN

Emily's life just wasn't getting any better. They lost the game last night, and everyone said it was because their second-string running back missed several big plays, and Drake still hadn't come back home. Everything was her fault.

And she hadn't even had a minute to do any type of follow-up on Mackenzie Barnes. Not even this morning because she'd had to look over her notes for the Smackdown demonstration in just a few minutes.

The only good news was that Dr. Meeks had called Naomi and said he would bring Charley home that evening. Naomi and Timmy were beyond excited. So was Emily—she'd missed him, and so had Sherlock.

The Saturday homecoming celebration was in full swing, a Rock Harbor celebration of education in all forms. The entire four corners where Houghton Street connected with Pepin had stages, each with a designation for the town-wide party. On the community center grounds, a roped-off area served as an information center, with all of the day's events and locations listed.

Across Pepin Street from it, on the lot beside the hospital, was a built-up stage where the Ojibwa elders gave example lessons for the children who lived in the Native American community.

Locals milled about, going from one demonstration to another. The dance would take place later in the evening. All of the town's restaurants would do a lot of business tonight—that was for sure.

On the opposite side of Houghton Street, beside the Konkala Service Station, a stage had been built that held Rock Harbor history artifacts from Anu Nicholls, Dave's grandmother and the owner of Nicholls' Finnish Imports. And in front of the *Kitchigami* Journal office, the stage was built for the school's Smackdown demonstration.

Nerves tickled up Emily's spine as she clasped and unclasped her hands in front of her. Both of her palms were slick with sweat despite the coolness of the weekend. Even though everyone seemed relieved the celebration hadn't been canceled, most of the students were still treating Emily as if she had a bad case of the chicken pox.

"You'll do fine, honey." Naomi planted a kiss on Emily's temple. "Forget about everything but the facts. You know this."

Emily nodded. *God, please let this go okay. I don't think I can handle it if they make fun of me in front of the whole town.*

"Ignore the rest of them," she whispered. "You did the right thing. Your dad and I are very proud of you."

Emily had told them about the jacket as soon as she'd gotten home. The last thing she needed was for them to think she was keeping something from them. The sheriff would have been sure to tell them how the school found out about Drake. They'd both told her how proud they were of her for doing the right thing. It meant a lot that she had their support, but she still felt like an out-cast with everyone else.

Naomi gave her a quick hug. "I'm going to sit with your dad and brothers out front. Remember, this is just a demonstration. You're going to do great."

"Emily!"

She turned to find Caycie staring at her, wearing a frown. "Is it true? Did you tell on Drake?"

Her mouth went dry. "I didn't tell on him. I just pointed out that he was wearing that jacket in a picture in last year's yearbook."

Caycie's eyes narrowed. "So you *did* tell on him. When Trevor told me that, I didn't want to believe him. I thought you were cooler than that. I guess I was wrong." She turned away.

"Caycie, wait. I didn't mean to get him in trouble. Really. He could have borrowed the jacket or loaned it to someone else or lost it."

"Whatever, Emily. You told on him, and now he's gone." She shook her head. "You really *are* a goody-goody." Caycie disappeared in the crowd before Emily could muster a response.

What would she say anyway? What *could* she say?

Mrs. Kantola took the microphone and moved to the front of the stage. The art club had really gone all out with the stage setup for the mock Smackdown competition. Two large lecterns split the stage in half, each long enough for three people to stand behind with round red buttons portraying the buzzers. There were six members on the team, but for the purposes of the exhi-bition, there would be three on each team.

After Mrs. Kantola gave the spiel about the team, their win-ning streak, and a few other particulars, she introduced each of them. Emily's stomach tied into knots as Clayton McGovern took his place. She was next. She let out a slow breath while Mrs. Kantola read her stats: GPA, past competition record, etc.

"Miss Emily O'Reilly."

Emily moved toward her space on the stage. Only her family and Olivia's clapped. A few in the audience snickered and made some comments Emily couldn't make out from the stage. Her face felt hotter than ever. She tripped and nearly fell into the lectern, but her teammate, Clayton, caught her arm and helped her to her place.

"Thanks," she whispered as she fought not to run off the stage in epic embarrassment.

"You're welcome. Pull it together. Don't let them see that they're getting to you." Clayton straightened, staring at Mrs. Kantola even as he spoke to Emily. "Pretend they don't exist."

Emily let out the breath she'd been holding. Olivia was right. Naomi and Dad were right. Clayton was right. She had nothing to be embarrassed about—she had done the right thing. It was because of her that the celebration was even taking place. If anything, the kids should be thanking her, not being mean to her.

She kept telling herself that over and over in her mind. It didn't work—she didn't believe it any more than she believed she'd ever live down telling on Drake.

God, please help me.

Since the demonstration was for homecoming, all of the questions posed for the mock competition would be about Rock Harbor and its history.

"Name the famous captain from Rock Harbor who built the house that is now the Blue Bonnet Bed and Breakfast and tell us why he built it."

All six team members hit their pretend buzzers.

"Clayton McGovern," Mrs. Kantola called on him.

"Captain Sarasin built the house so his wife could watch for his return from sea." Clayton spoke clear and confidently, just like all the team had been trained.

Mrs. Kantola nodded and continued. "What is the current population of Rock Harbor?"

Again, everyone hit his or her red button.

"Betsy Montgomery." Mrs. Kantola called on one of the team members playing as competition to Emily.

"Current population of Rock Harbor is two thousand five hundred and ninety-eight."

The questions and answers came faster:

"When was the Rock Harbor Community Center built?"

"During the heyday of the Copper Queen mining era."

Further questions about who were the first residents of the Michigan town and what impacts of the Finnish and Cornish peoples were on Rock Harbor. "When was the Rock Harbor Community Church built?"

"In 1886."

"What was the Rock Harbor Inn originally?"

All the team members hit the button, as usual.

"Emily O'Reilly." Finally, Mrs. Kantola called on her.

"In the eighteen hundreds, it was a French trading post."

"Correct." Mrs. Kantola set down her papers. "That concludes our demonstration of the Rock Harbor Junior High History Smackdown team. We're always on the lookout for dedicated and inspired history students to try out."

Emily kept the forced smile on her face as Mrs. Kantola continued to talk about the team's successes and how it brought such honor and recognition to the school, and how they hoped to expand the program in the future to include the high school grade levels.

Come on, Mrs. Kantola, let us go. Emily stared out over the crowd of probably a hundred or so people. Most of their faces all blurred together, which was probably a good thing. Many of the students in the front frowned at her, blaming her. She could make out Caycie's and Trevor's disappointed stares from the stage.

Refusing to think about them, Emily stared over their heads to the community center's yard. And then she saw *her.* No doubts, no mistakes. She smiled at Emily . . .

Marika was still in Rock Harbor. As if Emily's life wasn't complicated enough!

Emily wanted to find Dad and Naomi to tell them about seeing her mother right away, but she'd had to go straight from the Smackdown exhibition to the SAR school demonstration. Her family had waved at her onstage as they'd left to head to the SAR school grounds.

Emily kept a tight hold on Sherlock's leash when he lunged toward a red candy bar wrapper blowing across the grass. Bree and Samson were already waiting with two other members of the search-and-rescue team. The training equipment was ready and waiting.

"Sorry I'm late," Emily said breathlessly to Bree. Sherlock went to touch noses with Samson. The bigger dog's tail swished happily at the sight of the puppy.

"Don't worry. The rest of us just got here." Bree patted Sherlock's head when he jumped up on her leg. "You and Sherlock are going to be the stars of the show. Since this is a demonstration, I want the students to see how quickly a puppy begins to know what is expected of him."

Emily zipped her jacket against the blustery October wind. "He didn't do so well on Saturday. He still doesn't like that fake window."

"He'll do fine. Have him crawl through the tunnel first. It will give him confidence. And then lead him along the balance beam. Keep the window for last."

Good advice, but Emily still wasn't sure Sherlock was ready. "Are we doing a mock search?"

Bree nodded. "I'll have you hide in the box."

Emily swallowed hard. She'd much rather someone more trained took the center role. She wrapped Sherlock's leash around her palm and led him to the tunnel. Bree called everyone to attention and began to explain the process of training a puppy. Emily kept her eyes on the ground. Would her schoolmates think what she was doing was stupid? They already thought she was nothing but a snitch.

She couldn't help but notice Caycie in the front row, but Trevor and Josh weren't beside her.

Bree put her hand on Emily's shoulder. "One of your own, Emily O'Reilly, is my star pupil. Even though she's young, she has a real heart for helping other people. She listens well to directions and doesn't rush ahead of what I tell her. She's going to demonstrate how far young Sherlock has come. He's only been in training a few weeks, but he's going to be an outstanding search dog in a few years."

Emily dared a peek up at Bree, who was smiling proudly. "Now?"

Bree nodded. "Go ahead."

In front of the tunnel, Emily unclipped Sherlock's leash. "Tunnel, boy!"

The puppy nosed at something in the grass. "Leave it," Emily hissed. "Tunnel!" She pointed at the opening.

Sherlock yipped, then dashed into the tunnel. She breathed a sigh of relief. For a second, she thought she'd be the laughing-stock of the school. Again.

The tunnel moved as Sherlock raced through it. She moved around to the other side and clapped her hands. Sherlock barked when he exited the tunnel.

"Good boy!" She slipped him a treat from her pocket, then led him to the ladder that went to the balance beam.

His tail held high, he sniffed the base of the ladder, then looked up at her. "Climb," she said. He put his front paws on the first rung, then whined. "You can do it. Climb!" Slowly, he began to scramble up the ladder. He paused at the top and looked back at her. She moved to the other end of the balance beam. "Come, Sherlock. Walk."

He delicately began to step along the beam. Two feet from the end, one foot slipped. He yelped and scrambled for his balance. Emily leaped forward to help, but it was too late. With a final yelp, he pitched to the ground.

Her heart pounding, she dropped to her knees beside him. "Sherlock!" He licked her face and whined, then got up, tail wagging.

Kids were laughing and pointing, and her cheeks burned. But Rachel smiled at her and gave Emily a thumbs-up.

"You can do it, boy," Emily whispered when they reached the wall with the window. "Jump!"

But the puppy put his tail between his legs and refused to even try to leap to the windowsill. Biting her lip, Emily glanced at Bree, who didn't seem embarrassed. But then it wasn't *her* dog that had messed up.

Bree walked over, then squatted down beside Sherlock. "Up." Her voice was firm as she tugged on his collar.

He put his head on his paws and stared at them with soulful eyes. Emily felt terrible. "What should I do?"

"Go hide in the woods. We'll do the search next. He does a good job."

"What if he refuses to come look for me?"

Bree gave her a little shove. "It will be all right." She turned to the crowd and raised her voice. "Remember, Sherlock here is just a pup, and he's a little shy in the crowd. We're going to demonstrate an actual search now. Emily is going to go just into the edge of the woods and hide. While she's doing that, Samson will demonstrate the training we put the dogs through."

Only too glad to be away from all the stares, Emily jogged toward the tree line. The scent of pine and fallen leaves greeted her when she stepped into the shadows of the forest. Where should she hide? At the edge of a clearing where students could gather to watch would be ideal. She thought there was one right along this path.

"Emily."

Her lungs squeezed, and she didn't want to turn around, but she couldn't help herself. She slowly turned to face her mother.

"Marika." Her voice was a strangled whisper. "Have you been following me? You need to stop. Dad said you aren't supposed to contact me."

Her mother was as slim and beautiful as ever. Her eyes flashed, and her full lips covered in red lipstick tipped in a smile. "I've missed you, Emily. And look how much you've grown. You're starting to fill out early too, just like me. The boys will start flocking around, if they haven't already. I could give you some tips."

Tips from Marika were the last thing Emily wanted. She grimaced at the observation and wrapped her arms across her chest. "What do you want?"

Marika shrugged, and she took a step closer. "To see you, of course. You can talk your father into letting me see you and Timmy. He listens to you."

"I don't want to see you! And neither does Timmy. You withheld his medicine so he'd get sick and Naomi would be blamed. What kind of mother is willing to hurt her own little boy like that?"

Hurt flashed across Marika's face. "Teenagers are so melodramatic. Timmy was fine. I knew it wouldn't hurt him. Not really."

Emily backed away. "He could have *died*!" Tears burned her eyes. "And what about the school?"

"What about it?"

"Did you set the fire?"

Marika straightened. "Oh, so now I'm an arsonist as well? You're my daughter, Emily. I expected at least a small show of affection from you. I've changed. I have something important to share with you. Some news."

Marika's words made Emily close her mouth. The Bible said to honor your parents, but what if they were dishonorable? What if they were criminals? What if your parent was willing to hurt you or your brother? What did God expect her to do then?

Leaves crunching behind her made Emily turn. "Others are coming. I have to hide before the dogs get here. And you need to leave me alone."

But Marika was gone, leaving only shuddering branches from a nearby hawthorn bush in her wake.

 **ELEVEN**

Emily laughed as Sherlock scrambled on the floor of the entry as she locked the front door behind her. "You silly puppy."

The house was silent. Dad and Naomi had already taken Matthew over to Grandma Heinonen's to spend the night. Bree and Kade's twins, Hannah and Hunter, were already safely at Anu Nicholls's. Timmy would spend tonight with Dave after the homecoming celebration. She'd only returned home to bring Sherlock back and to change clothes.

Sherlock raced to the living room, then to the kitchen, then to the back door with his nose in the air. He paused at each location, sniffed, then ran to the next. Then he started it all over again: living room, kitchen, back door.

Emily glanced into the backyard . . . Charley wasn't there yet. She'd hoped to see that Dr. Meeks had already dropped him off so she could love on him a little.

She knelt and called Sherlock to her. She rubbed his chin. "Looking for Charley, buddy? Don't worry. He should be home today." *God, thank you for letting him be okay. We all miss him, but especially Naomi and Timmy.*

She filled the dog bowl with fresh water, then headed to her room. Since she was alone and had a minute, she'd do some checking. Not research, because she could still hear Inetta's warning in her head, but just checking. It wouldn't hurt anything to just do some Internet surfing. She wasn't going to do any searching on Charlotte Tarver.

Emily's laptop key made a little clicking noise as she hit the Enter button. She was thankful that last month Dad had given her his old laptop to do homework in her room, but it was slower than slow. Right now, she didn't have all day. All she needed was to look for—

Sherlock barked from the hallway, as ferociously as he could.

Emily jumped, then laughed at herself. Sherlock probably saw his own shadow, silly puppy. She whistled for him.

But Sherlock didn't come and continued barking.

Her mouth went dry, so she couldn't whistle again. "Sherlock! Come!" She waited for a moment, but he still kept barking. She raised her voice and put more firmness in her tone. "Sherlock, come!"

He came into the room but whined as he stared at the door, in the direction of Timmy's bedroom. The fur on the back of his neck between his shoulder blades was raised.

Emily knelt beside him and rubbed his head. "What is it, boy?" she whispered.

He growled, low in his throat, his eyes never leaving the doorway as if he could see something in Timmy's room. See something that had his full attention.

Now her mouth was really dry. He'd never acted like this before, not even when playing tug-of-war with Charley.

Could someone be in the house?

She stood, glancing around the room. She spied her cell phone on the desk. Should she call 911? Or maybe just Dad? Emily remained perfectly still, listening.

Nothing.

Sherlock still stood at alert, his gaze trained on the door to the hall.

Emily's heart pounded like it would jump right out of her chest. She didn't hear anyone in the house, but she couldn't explain Sherlock's behavior. Obviously he saw or heard something she didn't. What should she do?

Sherlock raced from her room, barking like crazy, running straight for Timmy's bedroom. His nails scraped against the floor.

She didn't even stop to think, just ran behind him. "Sherlock!" If something happened to him . . . Emily turned into Timmy's room, fear converted into protectiveness.

Woof! Woof! Woof!

Sherlock growled at Timmy's Batman costume lying across his desk chair, the mask hanging upside down just at the puppy's eye level.

Emily let out a breath of relief and laughed. She had thought maybe it was Marika. "Oh, Sherlock, that's just Timmy's costume. It's nothing to be scared of." She reached out and touched it.

Sherlock jumped backward, then slipped as he lost traction on the slick floor.

She laughed harder. "Come on, boy, it's okay. Nothing's going to get you." But if she didn't hurry back to the community center, Dad or Naomi were going to come looking for her.

After a quick change of clothes, Emily shut her laptop and secured Sherlock in the backyard before locking the front door behind her. The sun was beginning to disappear on the horizon, so she jogged along Cottage Avenue at a pretty quick speed until she hit Houghton Street. Within seconds, she could make out the lights twinkling from the community center.

The community center was the most beautiful building in all of Rock Harbor, with really cool high ceilings and fun corners to explore. Emily loved it. Ginormous chandeliers greeted her as she entered. The decorations they'd set out earlier in the week actually looked really nice with the dim lighting. The low light also made it easier to avoid the kids who'd been giving her a hard time at school.

Emily moved among the crowd, looking for Dad and Naomi. She bumped into Rachel and her dad. "Hello, Emily. Bang-up job today at the History Smackdown exhibition." Mr. Zinn's fishing lodge was the corporate sponsor for the Smackdown team, and he never missed an opportunity to let the team members know he was always paying attention to their successes. No wonder Rachel felt like she could never live up to her dad's expectations. He was really tough to impress.

"Thank you. Have you seen my dad?" Maybe she could get away quicker, before he grilled her about the team's upcoming meet.

"I thought I saw him over by the refreshment table."

"Thanks. I need to find him."

Rachel stepped close beside her and whispered to her, "I've talked to a couple of people, and they understand why you told the principal about Drake's jacket. I know some people are being really mean, but the rest of us get it. I've been telling anyone being mean to leave you alone—it's Drake's own fault he's in trouble, not yours. Besides, the sheriff would have figured it out eventually with or without your help."

Emily smiled. "Thanks, Rachel. I really appreciate it." And she did. Rachel didn't have to do that.

Rachel grinned back and shrugged. "It's the right thing to do."

"Well, thanks."

"No problem. Now, go find your dad."

She made her way across the room.

"Emily."

She looked over her shoulder to see who'd called her name and ran smack into someone. "I'm so sorry." Emily looked at the man she'd clobbered. "Oh, Geoff. I wasn't looking where I was going."

Geoff Makinen worked cleanup at the SAR school while he worked his way through college at night. At least, that's what Emily had heard Bree say about him.

"Ought to watch where you're going." He frowned at her.

"I'm so sorry." What was his problem? He'd always been nice to her before. "Um, have you seen Naomi around?"

His face scrunched up. "No, and I don't care to."

What was up with him? Confusion held her tongue.

"Oh, she didn't tell you that she fired me this week, huh?" His tone was downright mean, matching his expression.

"No." Neither Naomi nor Bree had said anything. Then again, it wasn't really her business, but still . . . it seemed odd that they hadn't said something, even just a mention.

"Yeah, she fired me. Without cause too, I might add." He jerked his gaze over Emily's head, then turned and disappeared into the crowd without further comment. Very odd.

"There you are. We were about to get worried about you." Naomi gave her a quick hug.

So that's why Geoff had rushed off.

"Was Charley at home yet?" Naomi's eyes twinkled with excitement.

Emily shook her head.

"Well, he should be there by the time we get home." She smiled and grabbed Emily's hand. "Come on, your dad's grabbed us all some pullas and cider." Naomi wove through the crowd, leading her to a table where Dad and Timmy sat.

Emily dropped into the seat beside her brother. She nudged him. "Hey, twerp. Sherlock wanted to attack your Halloween costume." She shared the episode as she sipped the warm apple cider.

Timmy found the situation quite funny, but Dad obviously didn't. His eyes darkened for a long moment. "Honey, you should have called me. If you're ever in a situation that frightens you, call me."

"I know, Dad." She needed to tell them about seeing Marika at the SAR demonstration. Emily opened her mouth to tell them, but Timmy laughed at that exact moment over a text he'd gotten. She couldn't say anything about Marika in front of him. Not when he still had such nightmares about her. She'd tell Dad and Naomi tonight after the celebration, when Timmy was over at Dave's.

Her cell went off. She checked the text message . . . from Inetta.

are you at the center?

She texted back: **yes. r u?**

The band took the stage and began to play. Dad and Naomi got those goofy looks. Great. They *were* going to dance and embarrass her.

Inetta's reply came through: **meet me at the copper room**

Emily's fingers flew over her cell: **on the way**

She stood and smiled at her brother. "I'm going to look around. Let Dad and Naomi know when they get back, okay?"

"Can I have the rest of your pulla?" He didn't wait for an answer before pulling her plate toward him and grabbing the bread.

She laughed as she headed out of the main room and down

the hallway. And ran into *her*. Dressed in a red dress and looking glamorously beautiful. "Hi, honey. You did really well at the Smackdown. I am so proud of you."

Emily couldn't meet her gaze. "Thanks."

"This is a boring event. Want to slip out and get a mocha? I know how you love them, and no one will miss you."

How did Marika know Emily loved mochas? "No thanks. I—I need to meet someone."

Her mother's eyes swam with tears. "Aren't you ever going to forgive me, Emily? I've changed. Spend a little time with me, and you'll see. We can do so many fun things together if you'll let go of your grudge."

Emily gulped. Maybe it was time she just decided to forgive Marika and get over it. Hard as it might be. That's what everyone told her to do. Wasn't that what the Bible said to do? She cleared her throat and stared at her mother. "I have to go. I've got a SAR school demonstration."

Marika thrust a slip of paper into Emily's hand. "Here's my cell number. Call me later."

"There's a restraining order against you. You're not supposed to contact me or Timmy."

"You don't have to say anything to your dad about this. No one has to know."

Emily went hot, then cold. "You want me to lie to Dad?"

"It's not a lie. It's just not telling him something that might upset him."

Emily backed away. "You haven't changed at all." She rushed off to find Inetta.

All of the rooms in the community center were named, and each name had something to do with Rock Harbor, and each was decorated with a theme. There was the Snow King room done in all whites, even white carpet, with pictures of landscapes covered in snow. The Kitchigami room was decorated in various shades of green, and the photos on its walls were of forest scenes. The Ottawa room, which was Emily's favorite, was done up in Native American decor. The Big Sea Water room had varying shades of blue and pictures of Lake Superior. And the last room on the right was the Copper room, decorated with memorabilia from Rock Harbor's early settlement.

"Hey," Inetta said as soon as Emily stepped into the Copper room.

No lights were on in the room, and the streetlights shot beams through the window, casting shadows on the walls.

Inetta looked her over. "Are you all right? You saw your mother, didn't you?"

"You saw her too?"

Inetta nodded. "She seems determined to make amends."

Emily hunched her shoulders. Inetta just didn't understand. "I don't want to talk about her right now. What's up?"

Inetta pressed her lips together. "You haven't looked into Charlotte Tarver anymore, have you?"

Emily shook her head. She'd looked a few things up, but nothing about Charlotte.

"Good. I got confirmation that Charlotte Tarver *did* hire the investigator to look into me." Her face lost her usual smile. "Emily, the investigator she hired isn't exactly a good character. I've done a little background checking myself, and this guy doesn't play."

"What does that mean, exactly?" Emily twirled her hair around her finger.

Her cell phone buzzed. She glanced at the caller ID, saw it was Timmy, and pressed the button to ignore the call. He probably wanted to ask some stupid question he and Dave had come up with to annoy her.

Inetta stared out the window into the darkness. "It means I should probably tell your folks what's going on."

"No!"

Inetta spun and narrowed her eyes. "Why? What's the deal?"

How could she explain? "Olivia specifically asked us not to. We promised her." Promises were gold. If one was broken . . . well, there'd be no more trust. "I can't go back on my word. At least not until after her parents' anniversary party. It's only two weeks away."

Her cell phone buzzed again, this time a text message from Timmy: **where r u?**

"I don't know, Emily. This guy . . . he's bad news. He has a criminal record. Breaking and entering, petty theft . . . he threatened a couple of people before."

"Are you in danger?" Emily's pulse spiked. Maybe they should tell Dad. If it were for Inetta's safety, Olivia would understand, right?

"I don't think so. My friend spoke to the investigator, so I think it's all okay. For now." She crossed her arms over her chest. I've also got my friend looking into Charlotte Tarver. I'll have him see if there's a connection between Charlotte and Mackenzie Barnes." She narrowed her eyes again and pointed at Emily. "You be careful."

Emily nodded as her cell phone went off again. Had to be Timmy again. She pressed Ignore.

"I'm serious. If I find out you made so much as one call, I'm telling your parents." Inetta glanced out the window again. "I'm still not sure I shouldn't tell them now anyway."

"Just a couple more weeks. Once the Websters' party is over, Olivia will talk to her parents and then everything will be out in the open. Okay?"

Inetta sighed. "Okay. For now. But if anything else turns up with a dangerous feel to it . . ."

"I know. We'll tell them." Emily smiled. "Thanks, Inetta. I've got to get back. Dad and Naomi will wonder where I ran off to."

"I've got to head out myself. I'll call you."

Emily nodded and pulled out her cell to answer Timmy.

The missed call was Dad's cell number. Uh-oh . . . the rule was she had to answer her cell if Dad or Naomi called.

"Stay in touch with me on this one. I mean it, Emily."

Emily nodded and rushed from the room. Something serious was going on about Olivia and her adoption, and now that the homecoming celebration was winding down, she'd devote her energy to figuring out exactly what.

But first she had to see what Dad wanted. She hit the button to call him back.

She slipped into the main room to find the lights up and the band no longer playing. She moved into the room, waiting for the call to connect.

"Emily! Where are you? Is Naomi with you?" Dad sounded a bit frantic.

"No, she's not with me. I'm by the main door. Why? What's going on?" She glanced around at the people crammed into the main room. Parents held their children's hands tightly. Faces were drawn.

"Emily." Dad touched her shoulder, then pulled her into a hug.

She slipped her cell back into her pocket. "What's going on?"

"Have you seen Naomi recently?"

Bree and Kade, with Dave and Timmy in tow, made their way toward them.

"The last time I saw her was when you went to dance. Why?" A funny feeling filled her stomach.

"She's missing." Dad's face was as serious as she'd ever seen. "She got a call near the end of our dance, so I went to get us some punch. She had moved by the time I got back." He ran a hand over his head. "She doesn't answer her cell, she's not in the ladies' room, and no one has seen her since. It's like she just disappeared."

Bree laid a hand on Dad's shoulder. "We'll find her, Donovan."

Naomi . . . missing?

Emily's heart free-fell to her toes. Where was Naomi?

TWELVE

This couldn't be happening! It was as if Naomi had just disappeared into thin air.

Emily paced the green carpet of the Kitchigami room as Sheriff Kaleva took notes, while Dad answered questions about the last time he saw Naomi. The townspeople had searched the entire community center, but Naomi was nowhere to be found.

She couldn't have just vanished.

Bree burst into the room and spoke to Dad, and then went straight to Emily. "Kade's dropping Timmy and Dave over at Anu's, then running by the house to pick up Samson for me. We'll start a search for her." She put an arm around Emily, bringing the pacing to a halt, and pulled her to her side. "We'll find her."

"Had she had any arguments or disagreements with anyone recently?" the sheriff asked.

Bree led Emily to a chair. "We had to let an employee go at the SAR school this week. Naomi's the one who actually fired him. Geoff. Geoff Makinen."

"He's here. I saw him." Emily jumped up from the chair she'd just sat in. "And he's really upset with Naomi."

"He told you that?" Dad asked.

She nodded her head and told them about running into Geoff. "He must've seen Naomi coming because he left right before she found me."

Sheriff Kaleva wrote furiously on his notebook before looking back at Bree. "Had he made any threats?"

"Not exactly, but he'd told several people that we fired him without cause. He'd told them that he was going to get us back."

"That's a threat, Bree." Sheriff Kaleva shook his head. "You didn't tell me?"

"I thought he was just full of hot air and he'd calm down after a few days."

Deputy Montgomery entered the room. "Sheriff, the woman reporter, Inetta Harris, is outside. She heard Naomi was missing and wants to talk to you."

The sheriff frowned. "Tell Harris I'll talk to her in about fifteen minutes. I want you to see if Geoff Makinen is still here. I want to talk to him."

Deputy Montgomery nodded. "And if he isn't?"

"Find him and bring him in for questioning." Sheriff Kaleva turned back to Bree and Dad. "Anybody else?"

Bree shook her head.

"The waitress at the Copper Club." Dad rubbed his face with both hands. "I can't remember her name right now, but Naomi said the woman had accused her of looking down on the waitresses and spouting religion at them."

"Odetta Sayers," Bree offered. "Some of us ladies at church made up a baked goods basket for them and included some

Scripture cards along with church brochures and invitations. Naomi and I delivered it. She said Odetta misunderstood and seemed upset by it."

"She was more than upset. She was angry." Emily couldn't believe she'd spoken aloud.

"How do you know?" Dad asked.

"I was there when Odetta talked to Naomi in the parking lot." She tried to lick her lips, but her mouth was too dry. "It was when we left the school after the fire. Odetta basically told Naomi to stay away from them . . . that they didn't need her or the church or the baked goods."

Sheriff Kaleva flipped pages in his notebook. "Did anybody see Odetta here tonight?"

Emily shook her head, as did Dad and Bree.

"I'll have someone follow up with her." He tapped the pencil against the spiral of the notebook. "Anybody else have a beef with Naomi lately?"

Emily let out a long breath. "Marika's in Rock Harbor."

All three adults spoke at once. "What?"

She met her father's stare, feeling guilty at the pain easily readable in his eyes. "I was going to tell you tonight after the dance."

"When?" Sheriff Kaleva asked.

"She talked to me on the day of the fire and again today. During the SAR demonstration. I went to hide for Sherlock to find me, and she was in the woods. She's here too. I saw her about a half hour ago. She wanted me to go get a mocha with her, but I told her to leave me alone."

"Why haven't you told me?" Dad clenched his fists, letting them sit on his knees. "What else did she say?"

Heat filled her face as she played back the conversation, and Dad's face went red. "I'm sorry, Dad. I wanted to tell you as soon as I got here, but Timmy was sitting right there and he's still having nightmares about her, so I didn't want to mention her name in front of him. I should have pulled you aside and told you right then. And probably the first time too." A lump the size of Rock Harbor lodged in her throat. She told her dad what Marika had said about making amends. "But I don't have to talk to her, do I, Dad?"

"No, you don't." He sounded fierce.

Kade entered the room, wearing his work vest, with Samson on his heels. Samson immediately went to Bree and nuzzled her fingers.

Dad turned to Sheriff Kaleva. "If Marika has Naomi . . ."

Bree squeezed Dad's shoulder. "Samson and I will start searching right now." She glanced at her husband. "Got my ready pack?"

Kade nodded. "In the Jeep, along with Naomi's scarf that she left at the house the other night when she came to pick up Timmy."

Emily stepped forward. "I want to help. I can go get Sherlock."

Bree gave her a sad smile as she shook her head. "I'm sorry, honey, but that's not a good idea. Sherlock's just not ready, and I need Samson to be free to move quickly."

"Then let me come along and help." *Please, God, let Bree say yes. I can't just stay here and do nothing.*

Dad stood, shaking his head. "Not this time. I've called Grandma, and she'll meet us at the house to stay with you."

"But I can help Bree."

"It's not a good idea, sweetie. I'll be much quicker with just me and Samson." Bree snapped and Samson stood at alert. "You need to do as your father asks, Emily. He doesn't need to be worrying about you too." She gave Dad a nod, then she rushed from the room, taking Samson and Kade with her.

Sheriff Kaleva stood. "I'll set up a search party in the town as well. There're plenty of people who will want to help. I'll talk with the media too."

At least she could help with the search parties.

Dad dug his keys from the front pocket of his jeans. "I'll run Emily home and get her settled with Naomi's mom, then I'll be back to help search."

"I want to help. If I can't go with Bree, I want to at least go with you." Emily took hold of her father's hand.

"No. I want you at home, where I know you're safe."

"But, Dad—"

"And someone needs to be there in case Naomi comes home or calls," Sheriff Kaleva interrupted.

She knew the sheriff had said that only to pacify her, but when she looked at Dad's face, she knew she couldn't argue. He was too scared already.

Once inside the SUV, Emily could almost feel Dad's nerves across the front seat. His hands were so tight on the steering wheel that his knuckles were white. "You should have come to me immediately as soon as you saw Marika."

"I know. I'm sorry." How could she explain? Some part of her wanted to desperately believe that if she didn't acknowledge Marika was back, her mother would just go away.

"Are you sure she didn't say anything else? Make any type of comment about Naomi?" He steered the car onto Cottage Avenue.

"No, sir. She didn't mention Naomi at all." That lump in her throat suddenly felt as big as the state of Michigan.

He turned the SUV into the driveway, shining the headlights across the tail end of Grandma Heinonen's car. They'd barely gotten out of the car when Grandma rushed onto the front porch. "Any news?"

Dad shook his head. "Bree and Samson are out searching now. Mason's started a search group back at the community center. I'm going back there."

Grandma's face was whiter than Emily had ever seen.

Dad hugged her. "We'll find her, Martha." He turned and gathered Emily into a big bear hug, squeezing her tight. "Remember Grandma is Naomi's mother. She might need a little extra TLC until we get back, okay?" he whispered in her ear as he released her.

She kissed his cheek, drawing in the familiar scent of his cologne, the one Timmy and Matthew bought him every year for Father's Day. Tears burned her eyes as she nodded.

"I love you. Mind your grandma."

Grandma wrapped an arm around her shoulders as Dad rushed back to the SUV.

"Call us as soon as you know anything," Grandma called after him.

He backed out of the driveway with a little wave, then was gone. Grandma tugged Emily inside. "Matthew's already in bed. Would you like me to make you some hot chocolate?"

Emily shook her head. "No, thank you." What she really wanted was to talk to Olivia.

"Well, let me know if you change your mind." Grandma sat ramrod stiff on the couch, staring out the front windows. "Oh, Charley's back."

"Really?" Emily rushed to the back door. In all the excitement, she'd forgotten Dr. Meeks was going to return him. She opened the door, and Charley and Sherlock both ran in, darting around her legs.

She dropped to her knees and hugged Naomi's dog while Sherlock licked her ear. Charley didn't look sick. Matter of fact, the way he was jumping around, he looked better than usual. She hugged him again. Naomi had been so excited to see him.

Tears burned Emily's eyes. She buried her face in Charley's silky fur. What if Naomi never came home?

God, please watch over Naomi. Keep her safe. We love and need her so much. Please, God.

She stood, wiping her eyes.

"Oh goodness, they're all wound up now." Grandma nodded at the dogs. "Maybe you should put them back outside."

Emily opened the back door, and the dogs ran into the yard to play, but not before Charley hesitated as if to acknowledge Naomi's absence.

She sat beside Grandma as the seconds slipped off the clock. Time seemed to pass slower than last period at school.

Five minutes.

Eleven.

Twenty-one.

Not able to sit still a minute longer, Emily jumped up. "I think I'm going to go to my room for a bit." She remembered what Dad had said. "If that's okay with you?"

"Sure, honey. I'm going to just sit here, close to the phone. You should get some rest."

The phone that never rang.

"I'll be in my room if you need me."

Grandma nodded, still staring at the silent telephone sitting on the coffee table in front of her like some shrine or something.

It was driving Emily crazy. She needed to talk to Olivia. Now.

THIRTEEN

"I can't just sit here and stare at the phone like Grandma. It's creepy." Emily lay back on her bed, clutching her *Phantom of the Opera* pillow to her chest. "She's not talking or watching the news or anything, just looking at the phone."

"Well, her daughter is missing. I bet she's really scared and freaked out. Think how scared you'd be if Sherlock was missing and there was nothing you could do." Olivia's voice sounded so calm over the phone. Just what Emily needed at the moment, somebody to be calm and sane when it felt like her world had turned upside down.

"Dad's really upset I didn't tell him about Marika." She should have told him. She should have asked to speak to him privately and they could've stepped away from the table with Timmy. Better yet, she should've told Dad about Marika on the day of the fire. She should have done a lot of things differently. If she had, maybe Naomi would be at home, making them apple cider and snuggling with Charley.

"Well, you would've told him tonight, right?"

"Well . . . maybe. It's a little late to tell him now, though." If Marika had Naomi, it'd be all her fault.

Just like Drake.

Because of her, two people were missing. Maybe she was bad luck.

"You can't change the past. As bad as Marika is, at least you know about her. Apparently, I can't even find out about my birth mother and my past."

"Inetta will uncover something. At least you know your birth mother's name." Emily stared at the clock on her desk. "Why hasn't Dad called?"

"They probably just haven't had time."

"Hang on, let me text him." Thank goodness for smartphones that could text while on a call. Emily quickly sent a text, then went back to her call with Olivia. "I sent a status update request to him and Bree."

"I've been praying, Em."

"Me too." *God, please let them find Naomi okay.* "Charley's home and he misses her, I can tell. It's like he knows something's wrong."

"Does he seem to be okay?"

"Yeah. Better than okay. He doesn't look sick at all."

A beep sounded.

"Hang on, I've got a text." She opened the message from her father: **nothing yet**

"Dad says there's nothing yet." Emily sat up, tossing the pillow aside. "I can't just sit here, Liv."

"You don't have much choice. It's not like Sherlock's ready to go on a SAR. We just have to keep praying and waiting. Want me to ask my mom if I can come over to hang with you for a while? I bet she'd let me."

But Emily's mind was already racing. "Sherlock's not, but Charley is."

"What are you talking about?"

"What you said . . . Sherlock isn't ready to go on a SAR."

"Right."

Emily glanced at the picture of her family on her desk, focusing on Naomi's smiling, sweet face. "Charley's fully trained."

"He just got back from the vet hospital."

"And he's perfectly fine."

"No, Em."

"I can use Charley and search for Naomi."

"Bree and Samson are already searching. You know Samson's the best there is."

"I can't just sit here, Liv. I'm going crazy. I have to do something."

"Your dad's already said no."

"But he's not here right now." If she could get Charley on Naomi's scent, she just knew he'd find Naomi. Samson was the best search dog, sure, but Charley loved Naomi. That gave him an edge.

"Your grandma's not going to let you go."

Emily reached for her jacket lying over the chair. "I don't plan on asking her."

"Em, you can't."

She swallowed. "I have to, Liv."

"It's dark out. You can't go out alone." Olivia's voice was softer . . . lower.

"I don't have a choice. And I won't be alone. I'll have Charley with me." She slipped on her sneakers.

Olivia sighed loudly over the connection. "Well, I'm not letting you go alone. Where do you want me to meet you?"

Light spilled from the windows of Bree's lighthouse. The wind was stiff here, fresh with the scent of water. "Liv?" Emily called softly. She kept a tight hold on Charley's leash with one hand and the mini flashlight in her other.

Olivia stepped from the shadows. Her hood was up, protecting her from the stiff wind blowing in off Lake Superior. "You sure Charley is up to this?"

"The vet said he was fine. Besides, he's missing Naomi. He'll heal better with her safe and sound at home. We're going to find her." *God, please let us find her.*

Olivia put her hands in her pockets. "Any word from Bree?"

Emily shook her head. "I texted her a minute ago. Samson has the trail and is heading down the beach."

"If Charley gets the trail, won't we run into Bree? Then we're both in big trouble." Olivia's eyes went wide.

Emily pressed her lips together. "All I care about is finding Naomi." Her eyes burned again. She would *not* cry.

"So what's the plan?"

Emily gestured with the flashlight to the north, toward the lake. "Bree is heading along the water toward her lighthouse. I thought we'd start here and see if Charley gets a scent."

"But we're likely to run right into Bree!"

"She's not this far yet. And she may never be. There's no sense in starting where Samson did. He's the best search dog out there. It's worth a try to start in the forest. There's a shack out there where Marika used to go when I was a kid." It made Emily sick to think about Marika meeting her man friends there.

"You really think your mom has something to do with this?"

Emily glared at her best friend. "Don't call her that! Naomi is the only mom I want. She's been the only real mom I've ever had." She was dangerously near tears again, and crying wouldn't find Naomi.

"Sorry." Olivia put her hand on Emily's arm. "I understand how you feel. Now more than ever."

At least she knew her birth mother, which was more than she could say for Olivia. "I'm sorry too." Emily scrubbed her eyes with the back of her gloved hand. "Let's just get to work and find Naomi."

She found the path to the trees behind the lighthouse and her grandmother's bed-and-breakfast. So far, no one seemed to have noticed they were gone. Grandma hadn't called for her or anything. She probably hadn't moved from staring at the phone.

The flagstone path quickly turned to rocks and dirt. "It's a ways in."

Olivia stayed close. "When were you there last? Do you remember the way?"

"It's about fifteen minutes from Grandma's house. The last time I was there, the raccoons had taken it over, and the roof was falling in."

Olivia stopped suddenly. "Then why do you think she might have taken Naomi there? It doesn't sound safe."

"She might not know that. I don't know where else she could be heading if the scent led this way."

"Maybe she was meeting a boat."

Emily bit her lip. "I hadn't thought about that." She looked back toward Lake Superior. Through the trees, she saw the moon glittering on the water. "At least we can try this. It's doing something."

Olivia got out her own flashlight and flipped it on. "Yeah, but after we check here, let's go home if there's no scent, okay?"

Liv was a good friend to come along on a mission she clearly thought was useless. If Emily had to sit one more minute and wait for the phone to ring, she would have gone crazy. "Thanks, Liv."

Emily shone her flashlight on the path ahead. "It's just through this clearing, I think. Here is as good a place as any to get Charley to search. Maybe he'll smell something."

She knelt beside the dog and unclipped his leash, then held the bag containing one of Naomi's socks under his nose. He took a deep sniff and wagged his tail. When he whined, she patted his head. "I know, boy. Search, Charley! Find Naomi."

He woofed, then crisscrossed the clearing with his nose in the air. He circled the space three times, then came back to press his head dejectedly against Emily's leg.

"That's okay, boy."

Something stirred in the shrubs. She tensed. "Anyone there?"

The hair on the back of her neck stood up, and the trees seemed dark and ghostly. Who knew what was in there? Mountain lions had returned to the Upper Peninsula, and they prowled at night. For the first time, she realized it might not have been a good idea to come out here at night without an adult.

Olivia clutched her arm. "Did you hear that?"

"I—I heard leaves or something." Emily listened harder. "It was probably just a raccoon or a squirrel. Let's try the shack." Eager to get away from whatever had sent her alarms flaring, she set off across the clearing. At least they had flashlights. And Charley. "Maybe they didn't come this far."

"Or maybe they didn't come here at all," Olivia said.

"We have to find her." Emily kicked leaves out of the way as she marched toward the old shack. It was still a few feet away when Charley's ears perked up. He barked and ran to the door of the wooden structure.

Emily caught her breath and raced after him. *Please, please let Naomi be there, God.* Charley nosed the door open and disappeared inside.

"Naomi!" Emily reached the opening and aimed her flashlight into the dark cavern of the building. The beam revealed only debris: empty pop cans, candy wrappers, a crumpled blanket, and shingles from the decaying roof.

Emily leaned against the door frame. "She's not here."

Olivia caught up with her. "But Charley smelled something. She's been here. Maybe he can track her from this point."

"Of course!" Emily called Charley to her and had him smell the scent article again. "Search, Charley! Find Naomi."

The dog whined, then turned to look around the empty space as if to say he'd been sure his owner was inside. Then he darted out the door with his nose in the air. Her heart in her throat, Emily ran after him. His tail began to wag, and he barked joyously before racing farther into the woods.

Emily's chest burned as she ran to keep up with him. She slowed a bit to yank at Olivia's hand. After the scare in the clearing, she didn't want to run the risk of anything happening to her best friend.

Her foot struck a root, and she tumbled to the ground. Olivia fell on top of her, and the last of Emily's air exhaled out in a painful whoosh. Olivia didn't move for a minute, then she groaned and rolled off.

Emily sat up and brushed leaves off her. She grabbed one of their flashlights from the ground. "You okay?"

"Yeah." Olivia got up and reached down to hoist Emily to her feet.

A scream sounded to their left, and Emily felt like her heart stopped. She tightened her grip on Olivia's hand. "W-what was that?"

"I think it might have been a mountain lion," Olivia whispered in a trembling voice. She reached down and grabbed the other fallen flashlight.

The unearthly screech came again, and both girls took off toward the path where Charley had disappeared. Terror seized Emily by the throat, and she imagined a huge cat with big yellow teeth and deadly claws. And what if it got Charley? If anything happened to Olivia or Charley, it would be all her fault.

Just like it was her fault Drake and Naomi were missing.

Her breath came hard and fast, and her lungs burned. The scream came again, but it sounded farther away. Her steps slowed. "I—I think it's going away." She shined the light from her flashlight at Olivia. "That was a close one."

Tears glimmered on Olivia's face, and she shuddered. "I never want to hear that sound again."

"Me neither." Emily cupped her hands to her mouth. "Charley!"

An answering bark sounded to her left, then the bushes parted and a dog raced toward her. Samson. And Bree, her face set and steely, came right behind him.

"We're in *so* much trouble," Emily whispered to Olivia.

FOURTEEN

"I can't believe you snuck out of the house alone." Bree dug her cell phone from her pocket as she glared at Emily. "And dragged poor Olivia and Charley out too." She punched on the phone, then stuck it to her ear. "What were you thinking?"

Words wouldn't form in Emily's mouth. The one person she looked up to as much as her parents, Bree, was very upset with her. And rightly so. Olivia still held tightly to her hand.

Charley and Samson rubbed noses, both tails wagging in the wind.

"Donovan? No, I haven't found Naomi, but guess who I *did* find out here in the woods by my house?" Bree continued to scowl at her. "Well, she's not at home with Martha. She's standing in front of me. With Olivia. And Charley."

She was *so* dead.

Bree pulled the phone about an inch away from her ear and stared at Emily with one brow arched.

Dad's ranting was easily heard. He was beyond furious. She'd be lucky if he didn't lock her in her room until she graduated from college.

Olivia squeezed Emily's hand, but it offered little comfort. She hadn't thought about what would happen if they didn't find Naomi and got caught. She'd been so sure Charley would find Naomi.

"I know, I know. What do you want me to do?" Bree snapped her fingers, and Samson moved to her side. Charley joined as well.

"I think both dogs had her scent but lost it. I'm sorry, Donovan, but she's not out here. She was, I'm sure, but is gone now. I'll bring Emily home." She slipped the phone back into her pocket, then pressed both fists onto her hips.

Emily wanted the ground to open up and swallow her. She was an epic failure.

"Your dad has enough to worry about right now, and you pull this stunt? Seriously, Emily, what were you thinking?"

Tears burned Emily's eyes. "I couldn't just sit at home and stare at the phone like Grandma. I needed to be out here. Doing something." A sob caught in her throat. "It's my fault she was taken anyway. If I'd told them earlier about seeing Marika, they would've been more careful and Naomi wouldn't be missing."

She couldn't fight the tears anymore. "I'm sorry I disobeyed and snuck out, and I'm sorry I've worried Dad more, but I love Naomi. She's my mom. I have to do something."

Bree crossed the space between them and pulled her into a hug. "Shh. It's not your fault Naomi's missing. Not in the least." She squeezed Emily to her.

Emily welcomed the affection but stepped out of the embrace. "I didn't tell them I'd seen Marika. I should have."

"Yes, you should have. If you had to do it again, you probably would. But it's okay, Emily. We don't know Marika is involved in Naomi's disappearance. No matter, you are not responsible for

Naomi being missing—whatever or whoever is preventing her from being here is what's responsible. Not you."

"I don't want her back in my life," Emily whispered. "Is she going to follow me forever?"

"She'll always be your mother." Bree's words were gentle.

"Naomi is my *real* mother. She's the only one who cares about me." Emily rubbed her eyes with the back of her hand. "And now Marika's asking me to forgive her. It's crazy."

Bree touched her arm. "Well, honey, you do need to forgive her."

Emily stared at her. "I don't want her around. Not ever. I don't trust her."

"It doesn't matter. The Bible says you have to forgive her. It doesn't mean you have to let her into your life, but you need to let go of the anger you feel." Bree held up her hand when Emily opened her mouth. "Hear me out, Emily. Bitterness will hurt you more than it will her. God is the judge, not you."

Emily crossed her arms over her chest. "I don't want to forgive her. And we both know Marika's most likely the reason Naomi's missing. Marika has always hated Naomi. She's so jealous of her. Not just because of Dad and how beautiful Naomi is, but because Timmy and I love her so much."

Bree sighed and her eyes softened. "You heard Mason. There are several suspects. Geoff's definitely as much of a suspect as Marika since he was at the center and clearly, as you heard, blames Naomi for losing his job. And he's certainly more physically able than Marika. Then again, we could all be wrong and there could be a perfectly logical explanation for what's happened and where Naomi is."

Bree had a point. Back at the celebration, Geoff sure had been quick to leave before Naomi saw him.

"Until something is proven, don't just jump to conclusions. In my experience, it's best to wait for the facts."

"But we know for a fact Drake ran away because I told the principal about the jacket being his. He's still missing, and that is my fault."

"No, it isn't. Drake lied to the sheriff and then ran away. His choice, not yours." Bree sighed. "You did the right thing. He didn't. Stop taking responsibility for something you have no control over. You might not have done things exactly the best way, but trust me on this: you have no responsibility or control over someone else's actions. Okay?"

Emily nodded. Maybe she wasn't totally to blame.

"And think about what I said about forgiveness."

Emily swallowed. "Okay." *God, I can't do the forgiveness thing by myself. I'm going to have to have your help to forgive Marika for everything she's done.*

Bree started moving down the path. "Having said that, however, you know you shouldn't have snuck out. You or Olivia could have gotten hurt. Or Charley. That wouldn't have helped Naomi or your dad."

"I know." She kept the flashlight's beam pointed at the path in front of them, matching Bree's and Olivia's. They had to be careful not to stumble over the loose rocks half-buried in the volcanic dirt. "I was just really sure Charley could find Naomi. I didn't think it through very well."

Charley and Samson barked, tails in the air, and the fur on both of their necks raised. Both dogs focused at something in the density of the woods to the right of the path, right in the direction of the shack.

Bree moved in front of Emily and Olivia. "What is it, Samson?" she whispered.

The famous SAR dog growled low in his throat. Guttural. Deep.

Charley joined in, flanking Samson.

The hairs on Emily's arms inside her jacket stood at attention. Olivia reached for Emily's hand again and held tight.

Underbrush cracked.

Samson and Charley both growled and barked.

A teenager burst through the trees, his hands in the air. "Please, I'm not gonna try anything. Don't let the dogs bite me." He was scruffy and dirty and shivering in a thin coat.

"Sit." Bree snapped her finger. Both dogs sat and stopped growling. "Who are you and what are you doing out here?"

Emily gasped. "That's Drake Wilson."

Bree never took the flashlight's beam off him. "Emily, text your dad and tell him where we are and ask him to have Mason send someone to my house to get Drake. Put Charley's leash on." She kept her hand on Samson's head as she studied Drake.

"I'm not going to try anything. I promise," Drake said.

Emily quickly sent the text before snapping the leash onto Charley.

"If you do, I'll let Samson loose."

"No, ma'am. I won't."

"Okay, let's go." Bree shined the light down the path.

Emily followed Bree and the dogs. Olivia fell into step beside her. "Wonder what he's doing out here," she whispered.

Bree stayed at least three feet behind Drake but must have heard Olivia. "So, what are you doing out here, Drake?"

"I've been hiding in the shack. Some guys bring dates out here sometimes." He glanced over his shoulder at Emily as he jerked his head toward Bree. "She's right, you know. You aren't responsible for me running away. I am."

"Keep going." Bree pointed her flashlight's beam on the path. Drake turned back down the trail.

"Why did you? Run away, I mean?" Olivia asked.

"Because the jacket *was* mine, and I *did* break into the science lab at school, but I didn't set the fire. I ran away because I didn't think the police would believe me." He stopped and faced them. "You have to believe me that I didn't set it."

"It doesn't matter what we believe. Why'd you break into the lab in the first place?" Bree pointed to the path with her flashlight.

He turned and continued walking toward Bree's lighthouse, but spoke louder. "A woman paid me fifty bucks to break in and leave the lab door open for her."

"Whatever for?" Bree kept the light shining on the path.

"She said she was a friend of Mr. Potts, our science teacher, and she wanted to leave him a surprise."

Bree snorted. "And you believed her?"

Even Emily had trouble with that. "What kind of a surprise?"

"I don't know. I didn't ask. She just said they'd met at a party, and she wanted to leave him a nice surprise." He stumbled on a loose rock, then recovered. "I know it sounds stupid, but fifty bucks is fifty bucks, you know? I figured they were dating."

"Who was she?" Bree asked.

"Dunno. She never gave me her name. I should have asked." Car lights slithered through the trees.

Everything about this smelled fishy to Emily. "What'd she look like?"

"Never saw her."

As the group cleared the woods, light from Bree's lighthouse pierced the darkness. "Then how did you get your money?" she asked.

"She left it where she said she would, in an envelope taped under the slide on the elementary playground."

"How'd she know to call you?" Bree asked.

"I don't know." Drake hung his head. "I never thought about it. Never asked."

"Because fifty bucks is fifty bucks, right?" Bree shook her head and approached the driveway lit up by the lights mounted on the side of the lighthouse.

Deputy Montgomery exited the cruiser, the slamming of the door almost drowned by the sound of the waves. "Drake Wilson?"

Drake nodded.

"Come with me." He smiled at Bree. "Thanks. Mason said he'd update you later."

"Anything new on Naomi?" Bree asked the deputy.

"No. Nothing." He nodded at Samson. "I guess he couldn't sniff her out?"

"She was in the area but is gone now."

The wind blew harder, shoving the smell of the surf across the beach. Whitecaps crashed against the water's edge.

The deputy put his free hand on the butt of his gun. "Probably got in a car."

Bree shook her head. "Not in the woods around here. Samson lost the scent down the beach near the woods. Even with the tires deflated, there are too many rocks and no beach for a car to ride on."

Emily remembered Olivia's suggestion. "What if she left by boat?"

"Could be." Bree nodded. "That would make sense where Samson lost the scent."

Deputy Montgomery nodded. "We'll check around on that. See if anyone saw a boat in the area."

"Tonight?" Drake asked.

"Yeah. What do you know about it?" the deputy asked.

"That's why I wasn't in the shack. I'd heard a boat and went to check it out."

"Did you see anybody? Anything?" Bree asked.

"I heard the boat and headed toward the beach. By the time I got to where I could see, the boat was leaving."

"How many people were in the boat?" Deputy Montgomery asked.

"Two. One looked like a guy, and the other was shorter and smaller, like a woman." Drake shrugged. "But it was really dark, so I don't know."

"Did you hear anyone mention a name?" Emily gripped Charley's leash tighter.

"I didn't hear any names."

"What about the boat?" Bree asked. "Big, small . . . maybe one you've seen before?"

Drake shook his head. "It wasn't big. More like one of the speedboats than a fishing boat. I don't pay much attention to the boats around here." His gaze locked onto Emily's. "I'm sorry. It was dark and I couldn't see much and I didn't hear anything."

"Thanks." Emily pressed her lips together.

"We'll check it out after the sheriff asks you some questions," Deputy Montgomery said. "Thanks again, Bree."

"No problem." She rubbed Samson's head while the deputy led Drake back to his cruiser. "You can take off Charley's leash now."

Emily did. Samson and Charley both ran toward Bree's house.

"Come on, girls. Let me take you both home. Olivia, I'm assuming your parents have no idea where you are, right?"

Olivia ducked her head. "No, ma'am."

"I suspect you're both going to be grounded." Bree clicked the button on her key chain and her SUV's locks clicked. She opened the back and the dogs jumped inside.

Emily reached for the front passenger door. Not only was Bree disappointed in her and Dad furious, but the Websters would probably tell Olivia she couldn't hang out with Emily for a long, long time.

She'd really messed things up this time.

 **FIFTEEN**

"Grounded. Until Dad says otherwise, which could be until I graduate." At last, Emily had a minute alone with Olivia. "I can't go anywhere but school and school functions. I can't even train with Sherlock."

On top of that, Dad had made it very clear that if she didn't straighten up, he wouldn't allow her and Sherlock to participate in the competition. He probably didn't mean that, but with Naomi still missing, he wasn't in the mood for any argument.

Emily and Olivia sat on the wooden bench along the side of Rock Harbor Community Church facing the parking lot. Some members of the congregation lifted a hand in a wave as they got into their cars. Others called out to one another. Emily just tried to blend into the side of the building.

The city's church sat on top of Quincy Hill, overlooking downtown. Emily thought it was like a guard watching over Rock Harbor. She'd always liked the idea . . . it made her feel safe and secure. Yet a day after Naomi's disappearance, no one had a clue where she could be. Emily felt anything but safe and secure.

Pastor Lukkari had asked for special prayers for Naomi, and Emily had prayed, but it hadn't brought her much comfort. And she'd been struggling with that whole forgiveness thing. What if Marika really *had* changed? Part of her wished it could be true. It hurt to have a mother who didn't seem to care. If Marika had changed, maybe Emily *could* forgive her.

Even though the service had concluded several minutes ago, Dad was still inside talking to several people. Sheriff Kaleva and his wife, the mayor, had gone out of their way to speak to not just Dad but her and Timmy and Matthew. Thank goodness Grandma had taken Timmy and Matthew straight from service back home. Both of them missed Naomi something awful. It broke Emily's heart to hear Matthew crying for her this morning.

Many of the ladies from the church had brought casseroles over to the house this morning before church. Sunday lunches in the O'Reilly household were usually a time for the family to be together. Without Naomi, today would feel . . . wrong. Emily didn't even think she could eat anything, not even a *panukakkua*.

"I know what you mean. My mom freaked out, and my dad grounded me for a week." Olivia zipped up her jacket as another strong breeze shot across the parking lot and whipped around the church.

"Only a week?" A week was nothing.

More people exited the church and made their way across the parking lot to their vehicles. Emily couldn't help but feel a bit of anger. How dare they go on about their happy day while her entire life was falling apart?

"A week grounded from everything electronic: cell phone, computer unless it's for school, television, radio . . . everything."

"Seriously?" Emily would die. Everything electronic? She couldn't make it a day, much less a week.

"I know, right? Get this, Mom kept going on and on about how my sneaking out was so *deceptive*." Olivia huffed. "I wanted to point out how *deceptive* it was of her to not tell me I was adopted for fourteen years."

Another crowd of locals headed to the parking lot, some of the girls whispering as they stared back at Emily. Even though Drake had said out loud to anyone who'd listen that Emily had done the right thing and he was thankful to her, a lot of the kids in school still treated her like an outcast.

"Ignore them." Olivia sighed. "Anyway, I didn't say anything to Mom. Even though I'm dying to know the truth, I didn't bring it up. I just have to believe there's a reason they haven't told me."

Emily leaned against Olivia, bumping her. "I'm sorry, Liv. Guess I'm gonna have to do all the online research, huh?" She grinned the goofy smile that always made her best friend laugh.

It worked—Olivia gave a little chuckle. "Ha. Looks like you're stuck with all the research, and all communications."

More people spilled out from the church, some of them drifting closer to the bench. Emily lowered her voice. "Maybe once Inetta finds out some more information . . . speaking of, I wonder why she wasn't in church today. Have you heard anything from her?"

Olivia shook her head. "I meant to ask you that."

"Last I heard from her was when I saw her last night." Emily snuggled into her jacket as the wind picked up. "Now that I think about it, it's a little odd that she didn't call last night to get the scoop on Naomi's disappearance."

"That is odd. Have you tried calling her?"

Emily pulled her phone from her pocket. Olivia sighed wistfully. Emily chuckled. "Sorry." She punched in Inetta's number, then waited. The call went directly to the reporter's voice mail. She shook her head at Olivia and waited for the electronic beep. "Hey, it's Emily. Olivia and I are at church and wondering where you are. Call me when you can. Bye." She slipped the phone back into her pocket.

"Maybe she's sick. I heard Dr. Parker tell someone there'd been a lot of people with strep throat recently."

"I guess." Emily turned her back to the church members talking loudly along the building. "She seemed fine last night. More than fine."

Olivia crossed her arms over her chest. "She'll probably call you back before you even get home."

"Maybe." But it was very unlike Inetta. Last night she'd met with Sheriff Kaleva, and from what Grandma had told her, Inetta had spoken on the newscast about Naomi being missing. Why hadn't she called Emily?

"Don't let your imagination get away from you, Em." Olivia's tone was firm, even though her expression mirrored Emily's worry.

"Okay, okay." She forced a smile, but made a mental note to call Inetta as soon as she got home if she hadn't heard from her. "So, *when* she calls me back, maybe she'll have more information on Charlotte Tarver."

"Hey, Emily." Lauri Matthews, Kade's sister, stood at the end of the bench. She was in town for a few days.

"Oh, hey, Lauri." Emily stood. She felt awkward next to beautiful Lauri, whose light brown hair shone under the October sun. "You remember Olivia Webster?"

"Hi," Olivia said shyly.

"Yeah. Hi there." Lauri turned her attention back to Emily. "I didn't mean to eavesdrop, but I couldn't help overhearing Charlotte Tarver's name. Are you talking about the attorney in Marquette?"

Great. Now she was going to get in even more trouble. "Um, yeah." She'd better think fast, before Dad came out of church. "For a research project we're working on." Which wasn't *technically* a lie.

Lauri cocked her head to the side. "Really?"

"Yeah." Emily nodded and licked her lips. "About adoptions."

"Oh. Then you're talking about the same attorney I was thinking of." Lauri stuffed her hands into her jacket pocket and turned her back against the wind. "Listen, don't talk to anyone at the Charlotte Tarver office."

"You know her?" Olivia asked, standing and crossing her arms over her chest.

Lauri shook her head. "I only met her once, when I was looking into options for my baby. There was something . . . off about Charlotte and her assistant."

"What?" Emily's curiosity radar bleeped.

"I can't explain it, really. Just that they seemed way too interested in me and the baby. And my family and support system. I don't know. She gave me the heebie-jeebies."

Kade and Bree walked out of the church, each carrying a smiling twin.

"Just use someone else for your project, okay?" Lauri gave Emily and Olivia a smile. "I'll see you later. I'm watching the kiddos while Kade and Bree join the search party for your stepmom. I'm hoping they find her okay."

"Thanks." Emily waited until Lauri joined Kade and Bree before she whispered to Olivia, "It's not just Inetta. Even Lauri thought something was fishy with Charlotte Tarver, and that was, what, five or six years ago?"

Olivia blinked her big eyes. "I'm starting to think maybe I should just forget I ever found out."

"Don't be silly. You—"

"Olivia! We're leaving." Mrs. Webster smiled at Emily, even though she had to be furious about Olivia sneaking out. "We're praying for Naomi."

"Thank you, Mrs. Webster."

Dad came outside, his eyes red. As she took in his pale face and stern expression, Emily felt like her tongue grew four sizes too big for her mouth. He looked so sad . . . so lost. She moved to hug him. He gave her a tight hug, then smiled back at Pastor Lukkari before releasing her. "Come on, honey, let's go home. I want to grab a bite to eat, then get out with the search group."

Emily knew she'd be left at home with Grandma and the boys. She fought the sigh as she followed Dad to the SUV. She gave Olivia a finger wave as she passed the Websters in the parking lot.

As much as she hated being left behind, she would have to stay at home and help Grandma with Timmy and Matthew. No way could she argue to go out now. Not with Dad and Bree both still pretty upset with her.

So she'd do what Dad told her, but she'd also figure out a way to discover everything she could about Charlotte Tarver. At least she could help Olivia, even if she couldn't help Naomi.

The house creaked as the wind whipped outside. Sherlock whimpered in his sleep, curled up in his plush doggie bed beside Emily's desk.

Emily stared out her bedroom window. The bottom half of the sun touched the tips of the trees in the forest across Pakala Street. Soon, darkness would swallow Rock Harbor. Another night without Naomi home.

Matthew had cried for Naomi a good twenty minutes before he finally fell asleep. Emily's heart had cried with him. Grandma had snuggled in bed with him, whispering assurances that his mom would be home soon. But it didn't seem to do any good. Even Charley's wet kisses didn't help.

There were no such assurances for Emily or Timmy. Both of them were all too aware of Marika's antics to get what she wanted. She'd messed with Timmy's insulin medication, which could have caused his illness or even death. Even now, she'd just assumed Emily and Timmy would want to see her . . . just because she was their birth mother.

Nothing could be further from the truth.

Emily turned back to her computer and stared at the search results. Maybe Olivia was better off not knowing about this Mackenzie Barnes. Maybe Olivia's birth mother was just as bad as Emily's, if that was possible.

But God changes people. The thought wouldn't let her alone. Maybe she should at least talk to Marika and see if it could possibly be true. She pushed her worries away. Better to concentrate on Olivia's problem.

She changed the search criteria, this time entering Olivia's birthday, county, and *births*. Seconds later, the results page loaded. She scanned the links, found the one to the state page, and almost clicked on it when something else caught her eye. A report of a missing baby.

Emily clicked on the link and rubbed her hands together

as she read. Although the house's heater had kicked on, a chill snaked around her spine. A baby girl, born the same day as Olivia, had gone missing her first day home from the hospital.

According to the news article, Mr. and Mrs. Carter woke up the morning after they'd come home with baby Grace, only to find their newborn missing. The police and FBI never found her. No trail had been left.

How awful! What if Matthew had been taken as a newborn? Emily knew her family wouldn't have been the same. She did further research on the Carter case, only to have the facts confirmed: someone had stolen little Grace and she'd never been found.

Emily twirled her hair. Fourteen years, never seeing the baby. Not watching her grow up. Not knowing what happened to her. It was heartbreaking to read how Mrs. Carter continued to push the FBI on the case every year, yet still get no results.

She closed the page on her computer, staring at the blank screen. If only she could research Charlotte Tarver without breaking her promise to Inetta. Especially after what Lauri had said.

Speaking of Inetta . . . Emily had been so busy helping Timmy with his homework and then helping Grandma get Matthew to bed and then researching on Olivia's birth mother that she'd forgotten to check her cell for any missed calls. She grabbed her cell from her jacket pocket. Sure enough, she had a missed call from Inetta several hours ago, but she had a voice mail.

Emily retrieved her voice message.

"Hey, Emily, it's Inetta. Sorry I couldn't take your call earlier. I'm in Marquette following up on something. I've got a meeting set with the sheriff tonight about your stepmom. I'll call you after I talk with him. Know that I'm praying for her safe return. Bye."

Emily glanced out the window again. The sun had all but

disappeared, leaving behind streaks of orange across the sky. Night would come in less than a half hour. She moved to the window. Sherlock lifted his head, then curled back up and returned to sleep. Emily stared out into the darkness.

Where is Naomi? Is she okay? God, please bring her home safely. We love her. We need her. Please, God. Please.

"Emily?"

Sherlock jumped from his bed, giving a little bark.

Emily spun. "Grandma, you surprised me."

"Sorry, honey. Just checking on you."

Making sure she was still in the house, most likely on orders from Dad. Put Matthew to bed. Make sure Timmy takes his medicine. Check and make sure Emily hasn't snuck out of the house again.

"I'm fine, Grandma." Emily hugged herself as she turned back to stare out the window. The wind howled outside. Sherlock plopped back onto his bed.

"She's okay." Grandma had moved silently across the room and stood practically beside Emily.

Throat tightening, Emily blinked. "You don't know that."

Grandma smiled. "But I do." She patted her chest, right over her heart. "I feel it in here. She's okay."

Mother's instinct? Emily didn't really buy into that. After all, Marika had never had any type of mothering instinct. More likely, Grandma was hoping.

"You don't believe me, do you?" Grandma asked.

Emily smiled. "I hope you're right."

"Are you familiar with Hebrews 11:1?"

"No, ma'am."

"I didn't think so. Hebrews 11:1 says, 'Now faith is confidence

in what we hope for and assurance about what we do not see.'"
Grandma sat on the foot of the bed. "Do you know what that
means?"

Emily shrugged. "Kinda."

"It means that we must have confidence in what we're hoping
for. Confidence that God will answer our prayers."

But what if God's answer was no? What if Naomi was never
found, like Grace Carter? She'd never been found.

"I see you have doubts on that." Grandma patted the bed
beside her.

Emily sat. "I just know that bad things happen, even to good
people, Christians who love God. Like with Marika. She hurt me
and Timmy." Her throat tightened again, but she pushed on. "We
were good kids. We loved God even then. But Timmy still got
sick. He could have died."

"But he didn't. And the good that came out of it was that
Marika was punished for what she did, and your father met and
fell in love with Naomi. Wasn't that a good thing out of something bad?"

"Yes, but . . ."

"But what?"

She couldn't explain. "I don't know. There are just bad things
that happen. Even if something good comes out of it, why does
the bad have to happen?"

Grandma kissed her temple and put her arm around Emily's
shoulders. "I don't have the answer to everything, honey, but here's
what I believe." She paused for a second. "I believe that because we
all have free will, we can step out of God's plan for us."

Emily wrinkled her nose. Every time someone talked about
free will, she got lost.

Grandma grinned. "Let me use an example. Think of God like your dad. You know your dad loves you more than you can imagine, right?"

Emily nodded. Even when Dad was mad at her, he always let her know how much he loved her.

"So, your dad makes rules to keep you out of harm's way, trying to protect you."

Again, Emily nodded. She might not always agree with Dad's rules, but she knew he didn't just make them to be mean.

"But you have free will, so sometimes you don't exactly follow his rules, do you?"

Heat burned up the back of her neck.

Grandma hugged her again. "It's okay, honey. We've all broken our parents' rules and got in trouble. And that's the example. What if last night when you snuck out, Olivia had fallen and hurt her ankle . . . would you blame your dad for her injury?"

"No." That was a stupid question.

"So when we break God's plans for us, acting on our own free will, and we cause someone else to get hurt, we can't very well blame God, can we?"

Emily slowly shook her head. She'd never thought about it that way.

"Something to think about, huh?" Grandma gave her another hug, then stood. "That's just what I believe, but it makes sense to me."

It did, actually.

"I'm going to put on a pot of coffee. I have a feeling your dad will be home soon and will welcome a fresh pot." She stepped toward the door.

"Grandma?" Emily stood.

"Yes?"

"Thank you."

Grandma smiled. "Anytime, honey." She shut the door on her way out.

Emily turned to the window again. This time she let hope fill her. Hope that Naomi would return to them safe and sound. Hope that Marika, or whoever was responsible for Naomi's disappearance, would be caught. Hope that the truth about Olivia's adoption would be uncovered and there would be a logical explanation for everything.

Hope that life would get back to normal.

 **SIXTEEN**

"I can't believe Dad's making me go straight home today. It's bad enough he made me come to school with Naomi still missing." Emily slung her arms through her backpack and slammed her locker door.

Olivia smiled. "Well, at least you could take Inetta's call and ask her to meet us at dismissal and fill us in on what she found out. I don't even know where Mom and Dad put my phone."

"That's the worst."

"I know." Olivia walked alongside Emily. They stepped out into the school's courtyard. It was still cold, but the sun filled the afternoon sky. "I got a lot finished on our Twinkie costumes, though, with no electronic distractions. They're really looking cute."

While Emily wasn't very crafty, Olivia could sew like a professional.

"Hey, you two." Inetta hopped out of her car as the girls stepped onto the asphalt of the parking lot.

"Thanks for meeting us here and walking us home. I can't

break my grounding, or I'd really be in hot water." Emily's face burned at the mere thought of Dad's reaction.

"No problem." Inetta fell into step with the girls. "I have a bunch to tell you both, so I'll talk fast. And don't interrupt, okay?"

They nodded.

"First, Emily. I heard from my source in the sheriff's office that they had a lead on Marika. Sheriff Kaleva has sent the deputy to follow up, and if the lead pans out, to bring Marika in for questioning."

"Where—"

"Eh, I said not to interrupt. That's all the information I was given and that was a few hours ago. I haven't heard anything else yet. As soon as I hear something one way or another, I'll let you know."

Marika . . . could she have already been picked up and Naomi already found? No, Dad would have come and gotten her. Since the elementary school got out thirty minutes before the junior high, Grandma would have already picked up Timmy.

"About the school. Sheriff Kaleva has gotten the phone records from Drake's cell phone. His story of a woman calling and hiring him to break into the school is plausible, based upon the records. There is an unregistered number on the record with the same dates and estimated times as what Drake claimed. The calls originated from a prepaid phone, so they can't find out who had the phone to make the calls."

They reached the intersection of Summit and Houghton and turned left. The church's steeple atop the hill seemed to point into the heavens.

"Right now, the investigation team is looking over the inventory of the science lab's chemicals, checking to see if there's any combination or something that grabs their attention. While everyone wants to believe Drake's story, they're having a hard time figuring out why a woman would set fire to the school. They can't find any motive."

"I know you said not to interrupt, but having been there when Drake was found, I have to say, I believe him," Emily said. He'd looked so sincere and earnest.

"And he doesn't have any motive to set fire to the science lab either. Not that we've heard," Olivia added.

The strong aroma of coffee seemed to seep out of the Coffee Place and cross Houghton. Inetta stared at the little shop like Sherlock eyed the steaks when Dad grilled. Emily laughed. "So they basically have nothing on the fire?"

Inetta shook her head. "Nope. They're hoping to see something on the inventory list that will give them a new direction. Until then, there's nothing else for them to do."

Emily chewed her bottom lip as they walked, letting the information sink in. Dead ends every which way.

"Now you, Olivia." Inetta returned Anu Nicholls's wave from across the street. "All the research I've pulled and everything an investigator friend of mine uncovered all point to the same conclusion that there's something *off* about Charlotte Tarver's adoptions. While there are several couples who sing the firm's praises on their adoptions, there are a lot more who refuse to talk to anyone about their experience."

"What does that mean?" Olivia asked as they stopped at the intersection of Houghton and Kitchigami.

Emily's street, Cottage Avenue, was next.

Inetta stopped and stared at the girls. "That means I'm going to be digging deeper for answers. You two don't do a thing." She wagged her finger at Emily. "I mean it. Don't so much as breathe

the name Charlotte Tarver. I think there's not only something off about some of her adoptions, but I think there might be a dangerous element as well."

Emily swallowed.

"I had pretty much made up my mind to at least tell your folks"—she nodded at Emily—"then your stepmom went missing. It's not the time. But you have to promise me you'll let me do the investigating."

"Well . . . someone overheard her name and told me Charlotte had creeped her out."

"What?"

Emily quickly told Inetta about their conversation with Lauri. "So it's not just you."

Inetta nodded. "Again, I can't stress how important it is to be careful. Especially for you kids." She stared at Olivia. "Are you *positive* telling them you know you're adopted would ruin their anniversary party surprise?"

"You promised you wouldn't say anything." Olivia's eyes were wider than wide.

"I won't. As long as you two promise not to look into Charlotte Tarver at all. Deal?" Inetta put her hands on her hips.

"Promise," both girls said in unison.

"Okay." Inetta nodded as a young woman stepped out of the Rock Harbor Inn and headed across the street to the Suomi Café. "Last thing, I have a lead on your birth mother."

Emily grabbed Olivia's hand. "Mackenzie Barnes?"

Inetta tucked a hair behind her ear. "According to my sources, she moved from Trowbridge Park about ten years ago. Her trail went dark right after that—no jobs, no bank records, no credit cards . . . absolutely nothing on her name, then three years ago, she pops up on the radar again. Employment records have her as a waitress at a diner just outside Marquette."

Olivia's hand trembled against Emily's. Could this be real? Olivia's real mother . . . living so close?

Emily stepped closer to her best friend and squeezed her hand. "Is that what you were doing in Marquette?"

Inetta nodded. "I tried to find an address for her but couldn't. I went to the diner to see if I could see her, but she wasn't working."

"When will she work again? Are you going back?" Olivia's words came out all in one long breath.

"I didn't ask." Inetta patted Olivia's shoulder. "If I'd asked for her, someone might have thought I would be trouble for her and would warn her. We could lose her entirely if she thought someone was searching for her."

"Why? Do you think she has something to hide?" Emily couldn't help but wonder if Olivia's birth mother might be a criminal, like Marika.

Inetta smiled. "Well, obviously she does have something to hide. The adoption was closed, so she apparently didn't announce she was having a baby and giving it up for adoption, right?"

"We shouldn't tell her. She didn't want me then. She won't want to meet me now." Olivia's eyes were filled with tears.

"You don't know that." Emily put an arm around her shoulders and hugged her.

"She gave me up." Olivia sniffed and wiped her face with her jacket sleeve.

Inetta handed Olivia a tissue from her purse. "Hey, we don't know anything. Because it's a closed adoption, there are no facts. For all you know, she might have regretted her decision and has been looking for you."

Olivia's face brightened. "Do you think so?"

"I don't know, sweetie, but I'm going to try to find out. Okay?"

Olivia nodded. "Thanks, Inetta."

Emily caught the time on her watch. *Rats!* "I've got to run. I'm late."

"I'll text you with what I find out." Inetta gave them both a hug. "Run, but don't forget your promise."

"We won't. Thanks." Emily jogged toward Cottage Avenue. "I'll see you tomorrow." She waved to Olivia.

She opened the front door to her house and was immediately met by Charley and Sherlock, tails wagging.

"Hi, honey. The boys and I are having a little snack of cheese and apples before dinner. Would you like to join us?" Grandma stood in the doorway, relief lining her face.

"No, thank you. I have some homework I need to get to." She paused, then crossed the room to plant a kiss on Grandma's cheek. "Any news?" she whispered.

"Not yet. Your dad called. His men's group from church is almost finished with their search grid. I made some soup for all of them."

Emily nodded, her hopes dashed. "I'll be in my room."

Sherlock followed her. She tossed her backpack on the floor beside her desk and flung herself across the bed. Tears wet her eyes. Sherlock jumped onto the bed and licked her face.

God, please, please, please bring Naomi home safely. Our family is falling apart without her. Please, God. Amen.

"Hey, can I come in?" Timmy asked through the crack in her bedroom door.

Charley pushed through before Emily could reply, his tail wagging as he touched noses with Sherlock.

Emily chuckled. "Guess so."

He shut the door behind him and sat on the bed across from her. He absentmindedly ran his fingers over the stitching on the bedding. Must be something serious he wanted to talk about. She waited for him to work out what he wanted to say.

"I want to know what's going on. The truth."

She narrowed her eyes. "The truth about what?" Had he been eavesdropping again? He had a really bad habit of it, and he was super curious—just like his big sister. If he'd heard her talking about Olivia being adopted, the secret would be out soon.

"Not you too. I'm tired of everyone keeping secrets. What's going on? What do you know about Naomi?" A frown filled his face. "Everybody stops talking when I'm around, so I know it's something nobody wants me to know."

Sherlock and Charley rolled on the floor, pawing at each other.

Emily chewed her bottom lip. She knew exactly what Timmy hadn't been told . . . Marika's involvement. Well, even if she wasn't involved, just her being back in Rock Harbor had been kept from Timmy.

Thinking about it now, that probably hadn't been the best idea. If he'd seen Marika without warning, he'd have really been shocked.

"Come on, Em, I know there's something." He used his puppy-dog-eyes look on her.

"It's not about Naomi, exactly." She let out a sigh.

"Just tell me."

"Marika."

His eyes widened against his quickly paling face, and it wasn't because of any pleading look of his. "M-M-Marika?"

Charley stopped playing with Sherlock and nudged his muzzle against Timmy's leg. Even the dog recognized the fear in her brother's voice.

She reached across the bed and took hold of his hand. "No one wanted you to know because of this reaction, Timmy. The nightmares you have, the fear . . . nobody wanted you to have to go through all this."

He didn't reply. Great, she'd messed up again. His nightmares would start again, and it'd be all her fault.

"It's okay. I'm a little shocked, yeah, but it's okay." He blinked several times, then his eyebrows shot up into his forehead. "Did she take Naomi?"

Emily lifted a shoulder. "We don't know yet. The sheriff is looking into it, but it's very possible." More like, very likely.

"Okay." He slowly began to nod. "Okay." His voice grew stronger as he pulled his hand free from hers and petted Charley's head until the dog was reassured enough to return to playing with Sherlock. "So what do we do about it?"

She pressed her lips together so she wouldn't laugh. Timmy wasn't exactly the action-taking type. He got sick a lot and wasn't very sturdy or active thanks to his diabetes. Then again, like her, he loved Naomi and would do anything to get her back.

"There's not much we can do right now."

His expression fell.

"I'm not keeping anything from you. It's not like that. I just heard that the sheriff got a lead on where Marika might be. He's sending someone to check it out right now. So there isn't anything for us to do." Her conversation with Grandma flashed through her mind. "Except we can pray."

"I have been." He nodded. "Do *you* think Marika took Naomi?"

What could she say? The truth. "I think she's involved some-how." In everything—Naomi's disappearance and the fire. Maybe even Olivia's adoption.

Okay, that was really reaching. Her feelings clouded her judg-ment, but that's how she felt. Who could blame her?

"I think she did." Timmy wore such a stern look, it reminded her of Dad.

"Well, hopefully the sheriff will find her and question her, and then we'll know for sure." And hopefully Naomi would return home safe and sound.

Timmy nodded as he stood. "Thanks for telling me."

"No problem."

He gave her a quick hug. "Let me know if you hear anything about the sheriff."

"I will."

The door creaked as he opened it, and he called Charley out with him. Sherlock whined. She dropped to the floor to scratch under the puppy's chin.

God, please, for all of our sakes, bring Naomi home to us.

Her cell phone buzzed. She grabbed it from the desk and glanced at the caller ID. "Hey, Inetta."

"Listen, I only have a second but wanted to let you know that they found Marika."

Emily's mouth went totally dry, and the butterflies went crazy in her stomach. "They have her?"

"She's in the back of a deputy's car right now, being brought into the sheriff's office for questioning."

"D—" She cleared her throat. "Did they find her alone?"

"Naomi wasn't with her. I'm sorry."

"It's okay. Did she say she knew where Naomi was?"

"All I know is that they picked her up just outside the city limits, she was alone, and they're taking her to the sheriff's office."

"Thanks for letting me know."

"I'll call when I hear something more. Bye."

"Be careful." Emily set the phone back on the desk.

Sherlock, obviously tired of being ignored, had curled up in his bed and his eyes were shut. She couldn't call Olivia and talk the news over with her because of her best friend being grounded.

Man, she really missed Naomi. Emily hadn't realized just how much she needed her until Naomi wasn't around.

She could vaguely make out bursts of laughter from the television in the living room where Grandma waited for Dad to come home. Was he at the sheriff's office, waiting to confront Marika? Would the answers come tonight? Maybe? Possibly?

Emily could only pray.

SEVENTEEN

"I still can't believe Dad left before I got up this morning." Emily slammed her locker and stared at Olivia. "I was so tired, I could only stay awake until ten, but I never heard him come home. And then for him to be gone before seven . . . and Grandma didn't offer anything close to information." Timmy hadn't even been able to eavesdrop because Dad left so early.

"Where'd your dad go?"

"On another search." At least, that's what she'd assumed.

"If he's still searching, then there probably wasn't much information to share." Olivia grabbed her lunch from her locker. "You didn't ask your grandma?"

The girls joined the crowd heading to the cafeteria along with all the other eighth graders.

"I don't think she knew anything. After all, if there'd been something important, she would have been excited or something."

"True."

"I tried to look online last night for any headlines, since

Grandma refuses to turn on the news, but my laptop's so slow, it's not even funny."

"You ought to bring your laptop to school and let Charles look at it. He's a computer genius, remember?"

"Okay." Olivia had a good point. Charles *was* a whiz on the computer. Maybe she had a virus or something he could find and delete off her system. "I'll bring it tomorrow."

"I'll tell him." Olivia stopped at the tables nearest the door. Kids plopped down at various tables. "Grab your tray and I'll hold us a place."

Emily headed to the end of the lunch line, her stomach growling. At least the line always moved fast.

"Hey, Emily."

She turned to find Drake rushing toward her. "Hi, Drake." Maybe since he stood here talking to her, the other kids would see and stop treating her like she'd hung him out to dry. A lot of them still whispered when she walked past.

So far, the sheriff hadn't charged him with anything, so that was a good sign. At least, that's what she thought.

"I've been looking for you." He flashed her a lopsided smile.

"What's up?"

"The sheriff asked me to work with a sketch artist to draw the boat I saw the night your stepmom went missing."

Her stomach tightened. "Yeah?"

He motioned her to step out of the line. "I thought it was kinda stupid at first. A real shot in the dark, but I wanted to help, so I did."

Just hurry up already. She nodded. The line was moving, and she was hungry. She'd been so upset about Dad leaving that she hadn't really eaten much for breakfast, even though Grandma made them oatmeal.

Drake stuck his thumbs into the front pocket of his jeans and leaned back against the painted concrete wall. "Well, last night they called me back in to verify something I'd described. An ornamental thing on the top of the back ladder."

"And?" *Could he get to the point? It might lead to Naomi.*

"I verified it, then was waiting to leave and overheard them talking. They got a hit on the boat because of the special ornamental thing. They were sending someone to go talk to the owner."

Hunger forgotten, Emily straightened. *Maybe this is what Dad rushed out for this morning.* "What time was this last night?"

"Almost ten, because my dad kept rushing the dude I talked with, saying it was a school night and all."

The timing would fit, considering Dad hadn't been home then. "Did you hear who the boat belongs to?"

He shook his head.

"Well, that's okay. At least it's a lead, right?"

He pushed off the wall. "There's more."

"What?"

"So, I was standing at the counter, waiting on my dad to finish talking to the sheriff so we could leave, when a deputy brought in a woman for something."

Emily kept her mouth shut. Marika? Surely Drake would get to the point in a minute.

"She was really hot, so naturally I checked her out." His chest puffed out a little.

Guys. She resisted the urge to roll her eyes.

"Someone asked her a question, and she answered, and that's when it went crazy." His face was shiny with excitement.

"What went crazy?"

"Her voice. I recognized it."

Ooooo-kay. Her stomach clenched.

His grin went so wide, it was no longer lopsided. "It was her. The woman who hired me to break into the school."

"You're sure?" Her voice shook a little, but maybe he wouldn't notice.

"Well, I told the deputy I recognized her voice. He got the sheriff, who made me tell him again that I was sure it was her voice. I'm 100 percent. It's a throaty, sexy voice. Hard to miss."

Emily felt a hardening in the pit of her gut. "So what did she say?"

"I don't know. They took her back to question her, then me and my dad left."

"So you don't know anything more?"

Drake grinned again. "Just her name. It's as sexy as her voice."

Heat spread inside Emily's chest, and she had to force herself to breathe. *Don't say her name. Don't let it be her.*

"Marika."

"Sorry for just showing up here like this." Inetta met Emily and Olivia in the school's parking lot. "I needed to talk with you two, and since one of you is grounded from going anywhere and the other is grounded from the phone . . ."

"Yeah, tell me about it. I'm sick of being grounded, and I'm only on day two." Olivia slouched against Inetta's Bug.

The breeze kicked loose leaves across the school's courtyard. Even though the sun shone brightly, the temperature had dropped quite drastically since that morning. With the wind chill factor, it was downright cold.

"Come on, let's start walking so Emily doesn't get in trouble." The flap of Inetta's coat bent against the wind.

Emily grinned and led the way.

Inetta walked between Emily and Olivia, her steps matching theirs. "I went back to the diner this morning for the breakfast shift, hoping to talk with Mackenzie. She wasn't there. I chatted up the lady working, and during the course of our casual conversation, learned Mackenzie had been fired last night."

"Fired?" Olivia straightened.

"Apparently, she'd had a habit of coming in late or forgetting to call in. Several times she just didn't show up for her shift." Inetta nodded as they passed the bank. "So I got to thinking . . . if she's a waitress and out of work, she'd probably start looking for another waitressing job in the area, right?"

Emily nodded, as did Olivia.

"So I pulled in some favors." Inetta nodded at the café across the street. "The Suomi Café now has an ad running in our paper, the paper in Marquette, and in the county newspaper. Hopefully, if she's looking, she'll see the ad and come to Rock Harbor to apply."

"Smart." Emily grinned at Olivia, who stopped suddenly. "What?"

"You didn't tell them why, did you?" Olivia's face whitened as she stared at Inetta. "I mean, everyone at the Suomi Café doesn't know why you wanted that job opening, do they? They don't know you're looking for my birth mother?"

Inetta reached out and squeezed Olivia's arm. "Of course not, sweetie. I told them I was working on a piece and needed this favor, and asked to be told the names of everyone who applies. They know nothing beyond that." She let go of Olivia's arm and smiled. "The funny thing is, they actually *are* in need of someone temporary for the holiday season."

Olivia let out a breath in a rush.

"Can't you just look at the applications and get her address?" Emily asked.

Inetta shook her head. "There are privacy laws, you know."

Oh. Right.

"They can, however, give me the names of those who apply. If she does, we'll know."

"Thanks, Inetta." Olivia gave her a quick hug. "I mean it."

Inetta blushed. "It's not a big deal." She turned to Emily. "Now, Marika is still in custody. She was brought in last night for questioning regarding Naomi's disappearance, but there's an interesting twist."

"Drake recognized her voice as the woman who hired him to break into the school."

Inetta's mouth dropped open. "How—"

Emily chuckled. "Drake told me. But he didn't know anything more than that."

"Well, at least I get to tell you *some* news." Inetta grinned. "Marika kept to her story of denying she had anything to do with Naomi's disappearance. She claims she has no idea where Naomi is."

Emily sighed. She could just hear Marika now.

"Once they brought up her phone call and payment to Drake, at first she played dumb. But when they told her he'd just positively identified her voice, she clammed up and demanded her lawyer."

"She actually has a lawyer?" Emily's hands shook. Marika had threatened to take legal action to get custody of Emily and Timmy and take them away from Dad and Naomi for good.

Inetta shrugged. "I'm thinking it's probably the criminal attorney who handled her previous case."

"What does that mean, exactly? To demand her lawyer, whoever it is?" Emily needed to know why her mother would want to set fire to the school. It made no sense. Then again, a lot about Marika didn't make sense. Still, Emily needed to know—for her peace of mind, and Timmy's. Not to mention their safety.

"The sheriff can't ask her any more questions until her lawyer is present."

"So we don't know why she hired Drake?"

"No. Not yet." Inetta stopped them at the corner of Cottage Avenue. "I know it's frustrating, girls, for both of you. But we'll keep digging until we know the truth, okay? I'm not going to give up."

Emily hugged her tightly. "Thank you, Inetta. So much. For everything you've done and are doing for us."

Again, Inetta blushed. "Now get on home before you get in more trouble. I heard on the weather we have a chance of snow tonight."

Emily broke into a slow jog toward home. Maybe Dad would have more answers. No matter how late he was tonight, she was determined to wait up for him.

A blast of cold air snuck under her jacket's collar, confirming the weather forecast. Emily shivered as she slipped in the front door. Heat welcomed her almost as much as Sherlock's joyous barking and tail-wagging greeting. But one thought stuck at her as she headed toward the kitchen to see Grandma and her brothers: wherever Naomi was, Emily could only pray she had shelter from the snow.

 **EIGHTEEN**

"I have some news to share with both of you." Dad sat at the head of the table for dinner. It seemed odd, Dad being the only adult in the house.

Emily had gotten so used to Naomi greeting her after school each day and making conversation as she cooked dinner that the house felt . . . not just empty, but cold and lonely without Naomi's cheerfulness.

Grandma had gone to check on things at the Blue Bonnet Bed and Breakfast, after having cooked a big pot of soup. The house smelled amazing, with the enticing aroma of onions and peppers. Yet the rooms still had the depressing feeling, like the lights had been cut off in the middle of a party.

Grandma had taken Matthew with her, and now Emily understood why: Dad wanted to talk to her and Timmy alone.

The house seemed colder than normal, and it had nothing to do with the wind raging outside. She let Charley and Sherlock outside for their last run of the night and then sat down at the table. If the forecast held true, they may have a snow day tomorrow.

"What?" Timmy stared across the table. He hadn't let on to Dad that he knew about Marika being back in town, which was good for Emily. Dad would be mad at her, and she was already grounded.

Dad quickly told Timmy that Marika was in town and had been brought in for questioning. To Timmy's credit, he never ratted out Emily.

"Sheriff Kaleva spoke with Marika in great detail." Dad tented his fingers over his bowl. "It's his opinion that Marika had nothing to do with Naomi's disappearance."

"Then who did?" Timmy's voice sounded stronger than he appeared.

"We don't know yet, son." Dad moved his spoon around in his soup but didn't take a bite. "We do know that Marika hired Drake Wilson to break into the school the day of the fire."

Timmy's eyes rounded. "She set the school on fire? Why?"

"She claims she didn't set the fire." Dad took a sip of his water. Emily didn't miss the way he avoided looking them in the eye. "You don't believe her, do you?" Everyone knew Marika was a liar. And a cheat. And a thief. At least she used to be. Had she really changed?

"Sheriff Kaleva will continue questioning her tonight once her attorney arrives in Rock Harbor. He got a warrant to search the place she's been staying at the last few days, so they might find something there."

"What about Naomi?" Timmy changed the subject smoothly. Either he thought there was information about their stepmom, or it bothered him more than he let on to talk about Marika. Emily figured it was the latter.

The pain and exhaustion in Dad's eyes was clear. "They're looking."

"What about Geoff Makinen?" Emily asked. "What did the sheriff find out about him?"

"He hasn't been located yet. According to his roommate, Geoff had plans to go camping in the Ottawa National Forest this week since he'd gotten fired."

"He's missing? He's a suspect in Naomi's disappearance and he's missing? Why isn't the sheriff out searching the Ottawa?" Emily couldn't believe this. Why hadn't Inetta heard? She would have definitely told Emily if she'd known.

"They've called in the park services to help. Kade and the other rangers are searching for Geoff. The problem is, his friend didn't exactly know where he planned to camp." Dad took a sip of his coffee. "It'll just take some time to find him, but Kade will."

"What about Odetta Sayers, that waitress who was so mean to Naomi the day of the fire?"

"She's got an alibi. Sheriff Kaleva verified it."

Frustration squeezed Emily's heart. "So basically, they have no leads and no idea where Naomi is?"

Dad reached across the table and took one of her hands and one of Timmy's. "Look, I know we're all upset. We're all a little scared. And that's okay."

Emily couldn't get over how clammy Dad's hand felt against hers. She ran her thumb over his rough knuckles.

"But we're going to find Naomi and bring her home." His voice caught on the last word.

For the first time, Emily noticed the sadness in the creases around his eyes. She wanted to say something—anything to bring him some comfort—but she had no words.

Tears slipped out of Timmy's eyes. He sniffed and wiped at his face, but he couldn't stop crying.

Dad let go of Emily's hand to pull Timmy into his lap and hold him. Many nights, Emily had stood in the hallway and watched Dad hold her brother just like this, when he'd woke up screaming from nightmares about Marika. And now the only mother he loved, the only one who'd ever been a mother to him, was missing.

It isn't fair!

"Guys, I know it feels hopeless right now, but it's not." Dad's smile looked forced. "Do you think Naomi's disappearance caught God by surprise? It didn't."

"Then why doesn't he let her come home?" Timmy buried his face against Dad's shirt and sobbed.

"I don't have all the answers, son." Dad reached out a hand to Emily.

She took his hand. It was even clammier than before, if that was possible.

"It's going to be okay," he said again.

If only she could believe that.

"I told you I wouldn't forget to tell him you were bringing your laptop." Olivia nudged Emily as Charles approached their locker, wearing his glasses and a big smile.

For several weeks, Emily had suspected Charles and Olivia *liked* liked each other. By the way Olivia blushed at Charles's smile, it sure looked like she was right.

"Hi, Emily. Olivia said you were having problems with your laptop?"

She handed it to him. "It's going really, really slow."

"Is it just when you're on the Internet? You might have a slow connection at your house or need to upgrade your wireless router."

"Well, it's slow then, but the last few days it's been slow even when I'm not on the Internet."

He slipped her laptop into his backpack. "I'll look at it during computer lab today. I might ask Mr. Jones to help. Is that okay?"

"Sure." The keyboarding teacher was pretty cool, for an old guy. "Thanks, Charles. I appreciate it."

"Me too," Olivia added, then her face turned red. Charles blushed as well.

Emily pressed her lips together against the smile.

"I'll meet you back here at your locker after school to give you your computer back and let you know what we find out." Charles turned and headed toward the math classrooms.

Olivia stared after him.

This time, Emily didn't stop the smile. "You like him."

Her best friend's face turned redder. "Of course I like him. He's a nice guy. And he's doing you a favor."

"Uh-huh." Emily shut her locker and grinned at Olivia's ever-reddening face.

"Shut up." Olivia nudged Emily toward homeroom. "He's just a friend doing a favor for us. That's all."

"If you say so."

"I say so." Olivia paused for a moment. "I looked at the Suomi Café help-wanted ad in the paper this morning. I wonder if Mackenzie will apply."

"Smooth change of subject." But Emily was willing to let it go. She didn't want to embarrass Liv any more than she already was. "I didn't even have time to look through the paper this morning because I was busy helping Grandma get Timmy and Matthew ready. Dad left to go search with Kade and the other rangers early."

"Will the snow slow down the search?"

"I would think so, but Dad said Bree and Samson were going with Kade. That should speed things up."

"At least we didn't get a lot of snow. Just a good dusting." Emily didn't want to talk about the weather . . . not knowing if Naomi was indoors or out. It was better to avoid thinking about it entirely. "Do you think the ad will draw her interest?"

"I don't know because I don't know her." Olivia let out a growl-groan. "It's so frustrating. On one hand, I hope Mackenzie sees it and applies. On the other, I hope she doesn't. Does that make sense?"

Emily nodded. "I get it."

The bell rang, and they headed into the classroom.

The day dragged by.

Homeroom.

Second period.

Third period.

Even the clock hanging in the cafeteria moved as if peanut butter had been stuffed behind the face.

Fourth period.

Fifth period.

Sixth period.

Finally, what felt like years later, the last bell rang.

Emily rushed to the lockers, beating Olivia by a good three minutes.

"A bit anxious, are you?" Olivia asked as she opened her locker. Her hair shined under the hall lights.

"You went to the girls' room and brushed your hair, didn't you?"

The blush dotted Olivia's cheeks. "It got messy after gym."

"Uh-huh. Sure it did."

Before Emily could tease her anymore, Charles rounded the

corner and headed straight for them. He didn't smile like before, and he had the most intense expression. Was whatever happened to her laptop fatal?

"Hi," Emily offered hesitantly as he joined her and Olivia at the locker.

"I figured out what was wrong with your computer." No *hello, how are you*, nothing but business.

"Is it bad?" She closed her locker and leaned against the row. Maybe she could save up the money their extended family always gave her for Christmas and buy a new laptop.

"Let's talk in here." He opened the door to the library and let Emily and Olivia go in first. They stopped at the table closest and set down their backpacks.

Charles handed Emily her laptop. "You've picked up a track-back program."

She didn't understand. "Is that a virus or something?"

Charles smiled and shook his head, much like she did with Matthew when he asked something obvious. "No. You did a search, which loaded a specific page. The track-back program is triggered when you use the exact combination of search words and page selection. When you do, and the program is triggered, it installs itself on your system."

"How does it do that?" Olivia's brow was scrunched like when she studied history. "Did she click on something and approve it?"

He shook his head. "No, when you click on the page after using the exact right combination of search terms, it opens like a connection between your system and that page's. That system sends this program to your system without you even being aware."

Sounded complicated. And wrong. "Is that even legal?"

"Not really. Most of them are some form of spyware in that

they pull certain information from your system, like your programs and stuff, to market products to you later. But this one's a bit different. It's really good. I had to get Mr. Jones to help me go through all the code."

"How's that?" How could something illegal be really good?

"Well, when you open the connection between the systems, it's not pulling information from your system exactly. It's opening a program that pulls your registered information and activates a type of global positioning satellite."

Olivia let out a little gasp, and Charles smiled at her, nodding like an algebra teacher when a kid finally gets how to work an equation.

"What? I don't understand."

Olivia grabbed Emily's hand. "That means someone got your personal information, like your name, your stuff, and even your location." She looked at Charles. "Right?"

"Exactly right."

Emily's stomach started to churn. "You mean someone got my personal details and they know where I live?"

Charles nodded. "It's a complicated program, one I couldn't trace back. Neither could Mr. Jones. He suggested you take it to the police and report it as an Internet crime. While they aren't stealing anything, the fact that the program is there and sent back such confidential information is highly suspect. That's what Mr. Jones said."

"Why would anybody want my information?" She felt sick to her stomach.

"I don't know. But the best we could figure out is that someone is protecting some information, and you put in all the right search parameters that triggered this form of protection." Charles lifted his backpack from the table. "That's the best we could do for you. Mr. Jones really wanted to stress how important he thought it was for you to report this to somebody."

"Thanks." Emily stared at her laptop, and Olivia and Charles said good-bye. She'd have to figure it out. What had she searched for that would trigger such a response?

Her hands froze as chills rippled over her. Her only searches were about Charlotte Tarver and Mackenzie Barnes.

 **NINETEEN**

"Hi, honey." Grandma paused from chopping onions, tears in her eyes. Timmy and Matthew ran around the backyard, Charley and Sherlock nipping behind them. A happy scene, one that shouldn't be disrupted when they came in and now saw Naomi still wasn't here.

But that was the reality they were forced to face.

"How was school?"

"Okay." Emily reached for the milk and poured herself a glass.

"Guess what?" Grandma smiled.

"There's word?" A bit of excitement jumped in her chest, then dimmed immediately. If there'd been anything urgent, somebody would've told her before now. Grandma would've said something as soon as she walked in.

"Your dad called about an hour ago. One of the rangers found a makeshift campsite that hasn't been claimed. He said Kade was hopeful it was Geoff's. They're waiting to see if the camper returns around dark."

That little surge of excitement filled her chest as she took another sip of milk. "Well, that's promising." *God, please let this be the break in the case Sheriff Kaleva keeps talking about. Naomi's been gone too long, and we all need her home.*

"I think so." Grandma scraped the diced onions from the cutting board into the skillet with the hamburger meat. She turned the stove on and stirred. "But, more importantly, your dad said Anu would be by to pick you up in about fifteen minutes to take you to Bree's, so you'd better get you and both dogs ready."

The excitement returned. "We're going on a search?"

Grandma frowned. "No. Oh, honey, did I make you think that? I'm sorry. I should have been more clear."

"Then why is Anu coming by to pick up me and the dogs?"

"Something about training, and your dad will pick you up on his way home." She wiped her hands. "So you'd better hurry and get ready. Anu should be here soon, and you don't want to keep her waiting."

Emily gulped down her milk and ran to her room. She threw down her backpack and grabbed her dental floss. She grabbed her cell, dialed Inetta's number, then put the phone on speaker.

"Hey, Emily. I haven't heard anything back yet." Inetta sounded rushed. "I'll call you as soon as I learn anything."

"I'm not calling about that." Emily quickly told her about the track-back program. "I haven't even done any historical research for Smackdown in the past few weeks." Emily tore off dental floss from the little box sitting on her desk. "The only searches I've done are on Charlotte Tarver and Mackenzie."

"This is crazy." Inetta's voice was filled with worry. "Did your friend say when the program was installed on your computer?"

Emily tossed the used floss into the trash can by her desk. "No, but my computer only started going so slowly last week. That's when I did the first searches." That had to be the connection.

"Have you told your dad?"

"He's not home from searching with Kade and the rangers yet. And I'm not about to discuss this with Grandma."

"I don't blame you. Listen, would it be okay with you if I came by and picked up your laptop? I'll have a techie friend of mine do some checking and see what he can find out. It might be that we can trace the program back to the other system."

"Sure, that's fine with me." She hoped they could, because it freaked her out that someone had lifted her personal information. "I'm about to head over to the SAR school, but I can let my grandmother know you'll be by to pick it up."

"A search?"

"No." How she wished. "Apparently I'm going for training."

"Thought you were grounded?"

"I don't know anymore."

Inetta chuckled. "Hey, at least you get out of the house. Maybe this is a sign your dad's letting you off restriction." She cleared her throat. "I've got to finish this article I'm working on, then I'll run by and pick up the laptop, if that's okay?"

"Sounds good. I'll let her know. Bye." Emily disconnected the call and stared at her closed laptop. She was afraid to even open it now. What other information did the program steal that Charles and Mr. Jones hadn't found?

Creepy.

Charley and Sherlock began barking, and Matthew's and Timmy's happy voices bounced down the hall. Must mean Anu had arrived.

Emily grabbed the dogs' vests and her laptop. She met Grandma at the foyer. "Oh, my friend Inetta is going to drop by later and pick up my laptop. It's running slow, and she's going to have one of her friends look at it."

All true, although there *was* more she wasn't telling. And wouldn't. "I'm going to leave it right here for her." She set it on the table just inside the doorway, then called the dogs and attached their leashes.

"Have fun, honey."

Emily headed out the front door, both dogs pulling against their leads.

Fun? She wasn't sure she'd have fun again until Naomi came home. She'd walked two blocks when she rounded a corner and came face-to-face with Marika. Sherlock must have sensed her dismay because he pressed his nose against her leg. Charley whined and looked up at her.

Marika looked a little pale and drawn. Her eyes were sad. "I've been hoping to run into you. I wanted to tell you personally that I would never hurt Naomi."

Emily said nothing at first. *Forgive.* It was harder than it sounded. "I hope not," she said finally. "Naomi is a good person."

Marika nodded. "She is." Her lips puckered a bit as if she'd bitten down on tinfoil.

Emily took a deep breath. "I just want to tell you that I forgive you."

Marika straightened. "You do? Really?" Her smile widened. "That's great! Let's go get a mocha to celebrate."

"I have SAR training." She felt lighter, happier somehow. Even if she never saw Marika again, it felt good to release the anger she'd felt.

"Tomorrow maybe?"

"I'm not so sure about that. Not just yet. I really need to know I can trust you first." Her shoulders back, Emily headed for the SAR training ground.

Bree was right. *Thank you, God, for helping me do that. And thank you for being there for me even when I mess up.*

Emily *so* didn't want to be here. Especially not now that she had forgiven her mother. She wanted to get a chance to tell Olivia how she felt. And besides, how could life just go on with Naomi still missing? It felt wrong. They should all be searching for her, not milling around the training ground of the Kitchigami Search-and-Rescue Training Center. And it was *cold*. The October wind whistled through the trees and snaked down the neck of her coat.

She called Sherlock to her, but he was more interested in following his daddy Samson around than listening to her. "Sherlock!"

He looked up at her stern voice, then went back to touching noses with the big dog.

Emily sighed, and Bree laughed. "Let's get started with some training exercises."

All her pent-up frustration threatened to spill out. "Why are you even here, Bree? Why aren't you out looking for Naomi?" she burst out.

Bree held her gaze. "There's no scent for Samson to find, Emily. It's futile to be rambling around in the woods when we don't know where to look. I know it's frustrating to have to wait for the sheriff to uncover something, but our hands are tied right now." Tears pooled in her eyes, and she blinked rapidly, then looked away.

Emily felt awful. She touched Bree's arm. "I'm sorry. I know she's your best friend and you love her too." Her own feelings had blinded her to how this whole thing was affecting others. All Emily could think about was how much her family missed her.

Bree looked up again, her expression serious. "Believe me, if there was anywhere I could think to search, I would."

"I know. It's just so hard to hear Matthew and Timmy cry for her." Emily's throat closed. "I can't stand it."

Bree hugged her, and Emily buried her face in the woman's wool coat. She wouldn't cry. She had to be strong for Timmy and Matthew. And Dad.

Bree released her. "Let's think about something else for a little while. That was my whole point in asking your dad to let you come over. Even though you've been grounded—for good reason, I might add—I thought we could use the exercise." She smiled and gave Emily a little push. "Take Sherlock onto the balance beam. It will be good for his muscles."

"He hates it."

"I know." Bree smiled. "Samson did too once."

Reluctantly, Emily seized her puppy by the collar and dragged him toward the incline leading to the balance beam. He dug his paws into the ground and whined. "I know. But you can do it, boy." She urged him up the board, and he wavered on the beam, then put his head down and walked across it. "Good job!"

He gobbled up the treat she passed him. When she looked around to see Bree's thumbs-up, she saw only Lauri standing by Charley. "Hey, where did Bree go?"

"She got a call."

Emily's pulse raced. "From the sheriff?"

"I don't know. She didn't say." Lauri pulled the collar of her navy down jacket tighter against her neck. "I'm ready for hot chocolate before the search training."

"Me too. I'm just not in the mood for training right now."

They turned to walk toward the school's main building, Charley and Sherlock on their heels. "I'm sorry about your mom," Lauri said.

"Thanks. We're going to find her." Emily infused more confidence into her voice than she felt. What would they do if they never found Naomi? How could any of them endure it?

She couldn't even think about it.

"Sure you are." Lauri paused and patted her dog Zorro's head. "He's getting rusty. I haven't trained him in forever."

"Is there a SAR group in Houghton?"

Lauri nodded. "But with my new job, there just hasn't been time."

"You got a new job? I hadn't heard."

"I'm a junior accountant in a new start-up firm. There's a lot to learn. The money's good though. I just bought Zoe a little computer tablet for games for Christmas. Not that she needs anything, really. But it feels good to finally be able to buy her something fun like that." Lauri smiled more to herself than at Emily.

"Zoe? You mean the mayor and sheriff's daughter?" Emily tried to recall something on the edge of her memory. She was just a kid back then, and the adults had shut up around her whenever Zoe's name was mentioned, but there was something . . .

Lauri nodded. "Your mom has probably mentioned I'm her birth mother."

Emily couldn't hold back a gasp. "You are?"

She eyed Lauri, who was all of maybe twenty-one or twenty-two. That would have made her sixteen when she got pregnant with Zoe. Only two years older than Emily was now. She couldn't even imagine that.

Lauri sighed. "I know. I was super stupid. My parents had died, and I didn't like my big brother Kade telling me what to do. I've always had a rebellious streak, and it really came out then. I can't say it's totally gone even now. I'm trying to be responsible, but it's hard."

Emily couldn't picture how hard that must have been for her.

"Don't do what I did, Emily. Listen to your dad and to God. Don't be taken in by a guy who says he loves you. If he loves you, he'll wait for marriage."

Emily's face burned at discussing such a subject, and she focused on the ground in front of her. Her dad would kill her if she even looked at a boy right now, and maybe that was a good thing.

"So what's it like to have to give up a baby?" She instantly clapped her hand over her mouth and then lowered it slowly. "I'm sorry, that came out all wrong."

Lauri grimaced and started for the building again. "Horrible. It was the hardest thing I've ever done in my life."

"Then why didn't you keep Zoe? I'm sure Bree and Kade would have helped you raise her." Bree and Kade loved kids. Surely they would've pitched in for their little niece.

"I wanted to." Lauri's chin jutted out. "In fact, I planned to. Then I thought it through. Zoe deserved a real mommy and daddy. I was still in high school. What did I know about raising a baby? And I might have been dumb, but I was smart enough to know I couldn't raise a baby. I was too selfish."

"Wow." Not many girls would admit their faults like that. Emily looked at her with new admiration. "So how did the sheriff and Hilary end up with her?"

"Hilary had lost babies during pregnancy several times. The chances of her having a baby were slim to none. She and Mason had a lot of love to give a child, as well as material things."

Lauri looked pensive. "The material things didn't matter as much as the love though. I knew Zoe would have an amazing life with them. And she has. She's good mannered, well-adjusted, and totally lovable."

"Yes, she is."

Emily and the dogs followed Lauri to the building for the promised hot chocolate. She'd never thought of how much self-sacrifice it might take to give a baby up for adoption. Was Olivia's mother the kind of person who had put her baby above what she had wanted herself?

TWENTY

Emily huddled in the scratch box and waited for Sherlock to find her. Her cell phone vibrated in her pocket, and she yanked it out to make sure it wasn't Dad calling. It was. Answering it was going to destroy the search, but she had no choice.

"Hey, Dad. Any news?"

"Kade has been trying to call Bree and can't get through."

"She has her phone charging in her Jeep. Want me to get her?"

"No, just pass a message along to her. We're searching a quadrant in the western part of the forest, and the sheriff just found a jacket we suspect is Geoff's. Grab Bree and anyone else you can find for a search."

Emily kicked open the door to the scratch box and avoided Sherlock's happy tongue. "Can I come too? I can bring Charley." Her dad hesitated for a minute. "Please, Dad! I'm going crazy."

"Okay, but I want you to stay close to Bree. Understood?"

"Sure. Where should we meet you?" She pulled out a pen and paper from her pocket and jotted down the meeting place. "We'll be there in a few minutes."

She scrambled to her feet and ran to get Bree. As soon as the SAR workers heard there was a lead, they split into groups of two and jumped in their vehicles. Emily left Sherlock at the SAR building with the receptionist and rode with Bree out to the parking lot of the picnic area. Her heart was thumping. Would they find Naomi today? She couldn't stand much more of this.

When Bree parked, Emily threw open her door and ran around back to get the dogs and her ready pack. Her dad waved from a group of people standing in the picnic pavilion. He was smiling, which was a good sign. When was the last time she'd seen him smile? She waved back and hurried toward him with Charley on his leash. Bree and Samson followed.

"What have we got?" Bree's tone was no-nonsense when they reached the picnic table.

His hand in a plastic glove, the sheriff held up a plaid flannel shirt. "This."

"I've seen Geoff wear that. His dog tore the hole at the elbow," Bree said.

"We hoped it was his," the sheriff said. "I took care not to contaminate the scent."

Bree held out a paper bag, and the sheriff dropped the shirt into it. "We've got several good hours before dark. Let's get going." She handed the bag back to the sheriff. "We're getting out there now. As the rest of the SAR teams show up, let them take a whiff."

She knelt by Samson and let him sniff the shirt, then unclipped his leash. "Search, Samson!" Her dog whined, then began to cross the open area with his nose in the air.

Emily called Charley to her. The dog trembled with excitement as if he sensed they might be close to finding Naomi. He plunged his nose into the bag, then barked excitedly as he ran around the clearing.

Samson stiffened, then ran for the woods. "He's got the scent!" Bree followed him.

Charley raced after Samson, and Emily hooted with joy and ran after them. *Please, God, let us find her.* In just a little while, she might be able to throw her arms around Naomi. If they found her, Emily resolved never to complain about watching *The Princess Bride*, Naomi's favorite movie, ever again. And she'd do dishes every night.

The woods closed around them, and the sounds of other searches fell away. Her chest burned with the exertion of keeping up with Bree and the dogs, and her feet kicked up the scent of pine and dry leaves as they went deeper and deeper into the forest. She scanned the forest as she went, hoping and praying to see Naomi's face.

A mud puddle was straight ahead, but Charley plowed through without pausing. Emily tried to leap over it, but her boots landed squarely in the mud, and she slipped and hit her backside. Her jeans were soaked through, and mud clung to them when she struggled to her feet.

The clammy cold made her shiver, but she brushed herself off and looked around. "Charley?" The dog had disappeared into the underbrush. "Samson?" She followed the paw marks in the mud and pushed through some thick bushes in the path.

This was the worst part about searching. She *hated* being alone in the woods. It was creepy out here with the wind rustling in the vegetation. She kept whirling to look, and there was no one there.

What if Geoff was watching her right now? Maybe he had a gun. She shied away from the thought because if he wanted to hurt her, it meant he might have hurt Naomi, and Emily couldn't bear that.

She cupped her hands to her mouth. "Bree!"

"What are you yelling about? I'm right here," Bree said from behind her.

Emily whirled with her hand to her throat. "You scared me to death."

"I told you not to fall behind." Bree looked her over and grinned. "Taking a mud bath?"

Emily made a face. "Not on purpose. Where are the dogs?"

Bree gestured. "Right through there. I told them to stay."

"Do they still have a scent?"

Bree nodded and took Emily's arm. "I think we're close. They're pretty antsy."

Emily shivered as the wind chilled her wet jeans. "We should have brought something of Naomi's with us."

"I have a sock in another bag, but I don't want to confuse the dogs with another scent. Not when they're tracking so well."

Emily stumbled over a rock and into a small clearing where the dogs sat. Charley rose and wagged his tail but stayed where he was after a cautious look at Bree.

Bree snapped her fingers, and Samson bounded to her side. She petted his thick fur. "Time to finish this, boy. Search!"

Samson barked and disappeared into the brush again. Charley followed, and Emily ran after him. Just past a stand of yellow pine, she saw the dogs circling a large tree. Samson leaped onto the tree and barked.

She frowned and stared into the tree. "Hey, there's a deer stand up there."

Bree nodded and strode to the base of the tree. A man's legs dangled over the side of the ledge. "Geoff, get down here right now. You've got a lot of explaining to do."

"Thanks for volunteering to take Emily home, Inetta. I really appreciate it." Dad held open the door to Inetta's VW Bug.

Stars twinkled in the dark, cloudless sky. No snow would fall tonight, but that meant the temperature would dip even lower. Soon Emily would be able to take a very hot shower and fall into her warm, cozy bed. *That* was a welcoming thought, even though it was barely six.

"No problem." Inetta winked at Emily. "I'd planned to run by the café and grab a quick bite. Is that okay?"

"Actually, that sounds like a great idea. I don't think Emily had dinner." Dad dug into his wallet and passed Emily a twenty-dollar bill. "Get something to eat and buy Inetta's," he whispered before planting a kiss on her temple, then straightening. "I'll be home as soon as we're done here."

Emily slipped her seat belt on as Inetta backed the car out of the sheriff's office parking slot, then took a left on Houghton Street, then an immediate right onto Kitchigami. "I'm glad you said something about eating. We went straight from training to the search. All I had to eat were a handful of Bree's pistachios, which are kinda nasty. I'm starving."

Inetta chuckled as she drove up the little hill to the Suomi Café. "Where are your dogs now?"

"Since he's just a puppy, Sherlock didn't go on the search. Charley was so tired that Bree took him home with her." Every muscle in Emily's body hurt. Exhaustion pulled at her arms. "We'll meet up tomorrow."

"Smart." Inetta parked outside the front of the café, then unbuckled her seat belt. "Let's get you something to eat before you fade away." She laughed as she stepped from the car.

Emily laughed as she followed Inetta into the café. Warmth immediately seeped over her. The yummy smell of grilled onions and french fries made her stomach growl loudly. As soon as she ate, she'd be sleepy. Good thing she didn't have any homework.

They selected a booth in the back, sliding across the cracked vinyl seats. A tall waitress appeared, her long blond hair pulled tight back into a ponytail that swung as she walked. "What can I get you ladies?"

"I'll have a cheeseburger and fries, with coffee, please," Inetta ordered.

Emily's stomach growled again. "I'll have the same, but with a strawberry shake, please."

The waitress scribbled on her pad, nodded, then bounced back toward the kitchen, her long legs pale under the uniform skirt.

"I just thought I was hungry before. Now that I smell everything, I'm so hungry I could eat a horse."

"No need to eat a horse. Your dinner will be here soon enough." Inetta chuckled.

"Did your friend find out anything on my laptop?"

"He confirmed what your friend and teacher already told you: that it's a track-back program. He's running traces to see if he can find out where the program came from. He'll call when he finds out something."

The waitress returned with a cup and a coffeepot. "Do you need cream?" she asked Inetta as she poured the cup.

"No, thank you."

The waitress smiled. Pretty, for an older lady. She was probably around Naomi's age. "Your burgers will be up soon." She moved to the table across the way to pour coffee for the older couple staring out into the night.

Emily rubbed her hands together, then blew into them. "It's just creepy that someone was able to put that program on my system without me knowing." She shivered. How much more information had they gotten from her computer? Personal information? She had a diary program she used at least once a week.

"It is. People who do that or hack into systems really scare me. I've toyed with writing a story about hackers."

"You should write something to warn people about trackback programs. I'd never heard of them before."

"I might have to do just that." Inetta tore open three sugar packets and dumped them into her coffee. She stirred slowly. "So, Geoff claimed he had nothing to do with Naomi's disappearance?"

Emily nodded. "He says he never saw her at the homecoming celebration except at a distance when he talked to me."

"Does the sheriff believe him?"

"Who knows? Dad wants to believe he knows something, so that's why he's waiting at the station while they question Geoff."

Inetta set down her spoon and lifted her coffee. "What do you think?"

Emily shrugged. "I don't think he knows anything. It was a good lead, I'll give you that. He had motive since Naomi fired him, he was angry, and his disappearance seemed too coincidental." She sighed. "But it was clear he'd been camping, and I saw no sign of Naomi."

The waitress returned and set the shake in front of Emily. "Here you go." She set a straw on the table, then moved on.

"Thanks." Emily took a sip of the shake. *Mmm.* Heaven on earth—sweet and creamy, with chunks of real strawberries. Just the way she liked it. "Although, as Dad said, Geoff could have put Naomi somewhere else. Charley and Samson didn't catch Naomi's scent there, and I trust their noses."

"What did the sheriff say about Marika?"

"Her attorney finally arrived this afternoon, so they'd just started questioning her before they really started the search for Geoff. They plan to finish questioning her now. At least, that's what Dad said."

If only she could know Naomi was safe.

"Here we are." The waitress set the plates on the table. The burgers smelled heavenly and the fries were piled high. She set a bottle of ketchup in the middle of the table, then filled Inetta's cup. "Can I get you anything else right now?"

"Can I get some extra mayo, please?" Inetta smiled.

"Certainly."

Emily refrained from sinking her teeth into her burger until they'd blessed the food, but took a huge bite as soon as she'd said amen.

The waitress returned with a bottle of mayonnaise. "Here you go. My name is Kenzie. You just let me know if you need anything else." She smiled again before moving to another table.

Inetta nodded as she spread the mayo on the bun. "New waitress."

"Yeah. I guess. Haven't seen her before."

"Does she look familiar to you in any way?"

"No." Emily stared after the blond lady, then looked at Inetta. "Should she?"

"Did you catch what she said? Her name is Kenzie. Probably

short for Mackenzie." Inetta raised a single eyebrow. "I understand she was just hired today."

Emily's hands froze, a french fry stuck in midair. She couldn't stop her eyes from trailing the waitress across the café. *That* was Olivia's birth mother?

Emily's heart hiccupped: the woman looked nothing like Olivia.

TWENTY-ONE

"She held on to her claims that she was never in the science lab at the school until Mason told her they'd found her prints at the scene." Dad took a sip of his coffee.

"I hadn't heard they found her prints." Bree leaned against the kitchen counter, staring into the backyard, where Samson played with Charley and Sherlock. She'd brought Charley and Sherlock back home that morning and stayed for Dad's update on Marika's questioning.

"Results from forensics had just come back late yesterday afternoon after her lawyer showed up." Dad nodded. "Got one partial and a pretty clear thumb that matched hers."

"How'd she explain that?" Emily had told herself she'd remain quiet, thankful that Dad let her stay for the conversation and not go with Grandma when she'd taken Timmy and Matthew to school, but she couldn't stop the question.

"She couldn't. Her attorney requested a moment, they whispered for a few minutes, then Marika said she'd been in the lab only for a brief time."

"Doing what, pray tell?" Bree's fists went to her hips.

"She said she needed a lab to work with some chemical compounds." Dad's tone was very even.

Emily recognized that tone. He knew something he didn't want to say.

"What kind of chemicals? Tell me she isn't involved in pharmaceutical stuff again." Bree shook her head. "And a high school lab? What was she doing?"

"We can't say for certain yet because she's not admitting to anything specific except what forensics determined."

"Dad . . . what's she involved with now?" Emily struggled to keep her voice from cracking. Fear lined her throat, but she knew Dad, and knew he had more information.

"She had refused to even answer why she was there until the crime lab came back with some trace components not in inventory in the school." Dad took a sip of coffee, then set it back on the table. "Apparently she needed to separate some pesticides. Remove the active ingredient and dispose of the inert components."

Pesticides . . . something about— "Dad, was she using pyrethrins?"

Dad didn't have to say a word. His facial expression said it all. Emily found it hard to breathe. "She poisoned Charley?"

"We don't know that, Emily." Dad's face stayed stern.

"Come on, Dad. What are the odds that Charley was poisoned with pyrethrin and then Marika shows up and is messing around with pyrethrins? This can't be a coincidence. No way." Emily shook her head. "You know that."

"It doesn't matter what I think or believe, Emily, it's what the sheriff can prove."

"And I just forgave her!" Emily burst out. Her eyes burned,

and she felt a keen sense of betrayal. "She said she'd changed, and I believed her."

Bree held her glance. "You did the right thing, Emily, even if she hasn't changed."

Her dad's brows went up. "You forgave her? What are you talking about?"

"Bree told me God doesn't like it when we hold a grudge and that I needed to forgive Marika. So I did. And it made me happy." She rubbed her forehead. "And now this."

Her dad glanced at Bree, then nodded. "Bree is right. But forgiving her doesn't mean you have to let her back into your life. You know that, right? She's still under a restraining order."

"I haven't gone anywhere with her or anything." The stupid tears blurred Emily's vision. Did she have to keep forgiving her mother over and over? How was she supposed to deal with this? "I think she poisoned Charley."

Bree pushed off the kitchen counter. "I'm going to go with Emily on this one, Donovan. That can't be a coincidence." She moved her fists back to her hips. "It infuriates me that someone deliberately poisoned Charley. Or any dog, really."

"What if it'd been Sherlock? It would've killed him." The familiar anger and bitterness rose in Emily's chest. Forgiving was hard when someone like Marika just kept doing mean stuff.

Maybe Olivia was better off *not* knowing her birth mother.

"I hope they plan to charge her for poisoning Charley." Bree crossed her arms over her chest.

Dad ran a hand over his face. "Unless she confesses to poisoning Charley, they won't charge her with that."

"Why not? Even if they don't have physical proof, there should be enough evidence to charge her."

"I think they're hoping to charge her with arson, which is a felony. Animal cruelty, while heinous, is a misdemeanor. Mason thinks he can make a much stronger case with the arson and use the poisoning as a secondary offense during presentation of the case."

Emily didn't understand all of that, but what she got was that Marika would get away with poisoning Charley. It wasn't fair!

Bree pressed a finger against her lips. "It still makes me furious."

"Do we have to forgive her for this too?"

Bree dropped her hand and sighed. "Yes, we sure do. But we can still be upset about it. We just can't hold a grudge. God forgives us every day for the things we do."

Emily pressed her lips together. "Okay." Poor Charley. Emily shifted in the kitchen chair. "Why?"

Dad looked at her. "*Why* what? I just explained why the sheriff wants to charge her with arson. A felony is a much—"

"No, Dad, I get that. Not that I agree with it, but I understand." Emily shook her head. "What I meant was, why did she poison Charley? There had to be some reason. What?"

Bree smiled. "Very good, Emily." She looked back at Dad. "Any ideas? Surely you and Mason discussed all possible scenarios."

Dad ran a finger around the rim of his coffee cup. "The only thing I could think of was she wanted Charley out of the way because she knew he'd protect Naomi, and without him in the picture, she'd have easier access to Naomi."

It felt pretty thin, even to Emily. There had to be more to it.

Sitting at the table, Bree squeezed Dad's shoulder. "I'm sorry, Donovan. She's still not admitting to knowing anything about Naomi's disappearance?"

"She swears she knows nothing about it. I want to believe her,

I do, but she's such a good liar." Dad jerked his attention to Emily. "Sorry, sweetheart. I shouldn't be discussing this in front of you."

"I'm a teenager now, Dad. I can handle the truth." Emily swallowed back the tears she desperately wanted to shed. But Dad and Bree were treating her like an adult, so she couldn't cry like a baby. "But Naomi was taken from the homecoming celebration. Charley wasn't around at all. Why poison Charley if she was going to take Naomi at a time when he wouldn't be there?"

"Opportunity, probably. Mason thinks Marika saw Naomi alone and used that."

"How does he think Marika got Naomi out of the community center without a struggle anyway?" Bree flipped a strand of her auburn hair behind her ear.

"He thinks she possibly ran to Naomi and said someone was hurt. Naomi would rush to help without checking." Dad played with his coffee cup and didn't look up.

Emily's heart pounded as she played various scenarios in her head. Her stomach knotted. "Because I wasn't there with you, Naomi, and Timmy, Sheriff Kaleva thinks Marika found Naomi and told her I needed her, doesn't he?"

"We don't know what happened, sweetheart." But Dad's voice said it all. That's exactly what they believed happened.

Which made Naomi's disappearance all her fault.

"I'm so sorry, Em." Olivia gave her a sideways hug in the school's courtyard. "I hate that Marika is putting you all through this nightmare."

Kids laughed and yelled at one another as they made their way to the buses and bicycle stands and parking lot. The afternoon sun teased them with its brightness while the wind struck chills down everyone's spine.

"No matter what Dad and Bree say, it's the only thing that makes sense, which makes it all my fault that Marika took Naomi."

"You really believe Marika has Naomi?"

"Yeah." Emily stared at her best friend. "Why? Don't you?"

"I don't know. I've only seen Marika a couple of times, but she's not very big. She's really thin." Olivia shrugged. "And Naomi is really strong and in great shape because of all the searches. I can't imagine that Naomi couldn't get away from Marika."

Beep! Beep! Beep!

Both girls jumped as Inetta stuck her head out of the car. "Come on."

They rushed to climb into the backseat, then Inetta slowly inched out of the parking lot. "I didn't know Rock Harbor had this many kids," she joked.

Olivia let out a slow, slow breath. "I'm suddenly really nervous."

"It's just to look at her." Inetta eased off Summit Street. "We can get the shakes to go if you want."

"No, it's fine." But Olivia's face had lost most of its color.

To change the subject and take Olivia's mind off her issues, Emily brought Inetta up to speed on what Dad had told her at breakfast.

"Wow, that's a lot to take in." Inetta parked in front of the Suomi Café and twisted to look at Emily. "Are you okay?"

"I'm fine."

Inetta flashed them both her sparkling smile. "Let's go drown our troubles in shakes."

They'd barely sat down when Tony, the cook, came to their table. "What can I get you this afternoon?"

"Three strawberry shakes, please." Inetta grinned at him. "Don't tell me you're having to wait tables along with cooking."

The elderly man chuckled. "Not at all. I'm just helping the little lass out while she used the facilities. She'll be along directly."

"Thank you, Mr. Tony."

He shuffled off to the kitchen.

"Where is she?" Olivia all but bounced in her seat.

"She's in the ladies' room, apparently," said Inetta.

Emily shook her head. "I don't think you look anything like her. Nothing."

"Maybe I look like my birth father." Olivia licked her lips several times in a row.

"Unfortunately, I do look like my birth mother." Emily bent creases into the paper napkin on the table. "Inetta, you knew Marika before she went to prison, right?"

Inetta nodded.

"Well, Liv pointed out something. Naomi's pretty strong and works out with the dogs and climbing. Marika . . . well, she's not exactly athletic. Do you think she could hold Naomi against her will? Or have taken her?"

"You know, that's a question I've asked the sheriff myself for interviewing purposes. Of course, I've agreed to keep most of our conversations off the record until he lets me know what's official." Inetta leaned back in the booth. "I can't see Marika going to the trouble it would take to keep Naomi. At least not this long. It's almost too much work for her, knowing how Marika doesn't like to stay around and do any actual work."

Wasn't that the truth? She'd left Dad when Timmy was a baby. "So you don't think she's involved?"

"She might be involved, or know more than she's admitting,

but if you're asking me if I think she's got Naomi, I'd have to say no."

"Back for another strawberry shake, are you?" Kenzie set a shake in front of Emily, a big smile on her face. "And you brought a friend this time."

Olivia stared at Kenzie. Not a polite stare either, but a rude one. The entire time she set the shakes and straws on the table.

"Thank you," Inetta said.

Still, Olivia said nothing. Just kept staring.

"Looks great." Emily stabbed the thick malt with her straw.

"Let me know if you need anything else." Kenzie tossed Olivia a final odd look, then moved to wait on other customers.

"Liv!" Emily nudged her.

Olivia shook her head. "Sorry. It's just . . . I don't know. I expected to feel something when I saw her, you know? Some type of connection or something." Tears glistened in her eyes. "I know it sounds silly, but I thought there'd be something, even a little thing. But there wasn't. She's a complete stranger."

"Hey, she *is* a stranger. This is the first time you've laid eyes on her."

Olivia looked across the café at Kenzie, then back at Inetta. "Are you positive it's the same Mackenzie?"

"Positive."

She shook her head. "I just can't picture her as my mother."

Kenzie came back by. "How're those shakes?"

"Yummy." Emily vowed at least she wouldn't be rude.

Inetta tilted her head. "You look so familiar to me. Are you from around here?"

Emily felt Olivia stiffen beside her.

"Not really."

"Hmm. I don't usually forget a face." Inetta stirred her shake with the straw. "I know I've seen you somewhere before."

The blush in Kenzie's face deepened a shade. "I'm sorry, you don't look familiar to—"

"Charlotte." Inetta snapped her fingers. "That's it. I've seen you at Charlotte Tarver's office. You know her, right? The attorney?"

All the color drained from Kenzie's face.

Inetta lowered her voice. "You had a baby you gave up for adoption, and Charlotte Tarver was the attorney who handled the adoption. I'm right, aren't I?"

"Who are you?" Kenzie wore a panicked expression.

"I'm a reporter, but that's not why I'm asking you this. I'm only interested because I'm helping a friend."

"Please." Kenzie looked over her shoulder, then back at Inetta, totally ignoring Olivia and Emily. "I just got this job. I need it. Please don't say anything."

"I'm not here to cause you any trouble." Inetta's tone was much softer. "I'm just trying to help a friend. A young lady who wants to know who her birth mother is. That's all."

Kenzie stiffened. "You don't know, do you? You think I'm some girl's birth mother?"

Inetta clasped her hands together and set them on the table. "Mackenzie, I know you're the birth mother. Your name is listed as such on documentation from the Michigan Department of Health. Baby girl, born July 13 at 7:09 p.m., fourteen years ago."

A bell rang, then Tony hollered out, "Order up."

"I've got to get that." Kenzie turned to go.

"Wait a minute." Inetta grabbed her arm. "I have more questions."

"Look, let me finish my shift and then I'll tell you what you need to know. I get off in two hours. We can talk then. Okay?"

Inetta nodded and released her hold on Kenzie. The waitress rushed off to the kitchen.

Inetta reached across the table and patted Olivia's hand. "We're going to find out what's going on."

TWENTY-TWO

"Thanks again, Inetta, for calling our parents and getting them to agree to let us stay." Emily still couldn't believe Dad and the Websters had said okay to Inetta's plea to allow them to help her with a story.

Emily checked her watch again. Mackenzie should finish her shift any minute now. Excitement had her knee bouncing.

The café had gotten busier with the early dinner crowd. The three of them had moved from a booth to the table in the back corner, farthest from traffic. Random conversations filled the air, combined with silverware clanking and glassware rattling.

"Well, it's the truth. I am working on a story, and I do need your help." Inetta smiled, then pulled out her notebook. She checked her watch as well.

"I'm so nervous. More now than before I first saw her. Isn't that strange?" Olivia took a sip of water.

"You just want answers, Liv. That's why you're nervous." Emily nodded.

"Sometimes I think maybe I should just leave it all alone, you know? Maybe I'm better off not knowing."

Emily couldn't say anything. Most times, she wished she didn't know Marika, much less have her for a mother. But forgiving her had made a difference, even if Emily knew they'd never be close. She had to believe that in some corner of her heart, Marika cared about her kids a little.

"Too late now. Here she comes." Inetta sat up a little straighter in the wooden chair. They'd put the empty chair between Emily and Olivia, across the table from Inetta.

"Thanks for waiting." Mackenzie's cheeks were rosy. "I really need this job."

"Tell me about your involvement with Charlotte Tarver." Inetta leaned forward and tapped her pen against her notebook.

"How much did she tell you?"

Inetta shook her head. "Why don't you just tell me the story and I'll see how it matches to what I already know?"

"I don't know what she told you, but I only participated that one July, not like some of the other girls." Mackenzie's nostrils flared in and out.

"You don't need to defend anything to me right now. Just tell me your side."

Emily pressed her lips together. Inetta was playing Mackenzie, making her think they knew something that they didn't. No wonder she was such a great reporter.

"Okay. I think it's time the truth came out anyway. I've been reading my Bible lately, and I know what I've done is wrong. I need to do what I can to make it right."

Inetta nodded. "Just tell me what happened."

Mackenzie let out a slow breath. "I was young and stupid

fourteen years ago." She smiled at Emily and Olivia. "Only a few years older than you girls look to be." She licked her lips. "I made some really bad choices. I got pregnant. The baby's father dumped me when he found out about the baby. My parents threw me out, and I was living in my car."

Inetta played with the pen. *Click-click. Click-click.* Emily understood . . . she wanted to rush Mackenzie along in her story too.

Mackenzie reached for the paper napkin. She crumpled it tight in her fist. "I first met Charlotte at the convenience store across town. I'd slipped in, intending to steal something to eat."

Her eyes filled with tears. "You have to understand, I was really, really hungry, and I knew I needed to eat for the baby."

Click-click-click.

"So I went into the store across town, far away from my crummy neighborhood so no one would recognize me. I'd managed to pocket two apples, and I knew I'd already pushed my luck. I headed to leave but saw a small pack of hamburger meat. It'd been so long since I had real meat. I couldn't resist." Mackenzie tore small pieces from the napkin, letting them pile on top of the table. "I almost had it in my purse when the cashier saw me and yelled."

Emily found tears welling up in her own eyes. How horrible to be so hungry.

"I ran, of course, but the cashier was young. He jumped over the counter and ran out after me. I nearly knocked over a lady on the street just as the cashier grabbed my arm." She shredded the napkin faster. "That woman was Charlotte Tarver, and after hearing the cashier threaten to call the cops, she paid him for what I'd stolen and he let me go."

Click. Click.

Mackenzie ran her fingers through her wispy bangs. "She took me to her office and told me she could help me. She told me that if I would give my baby up for adoption, let the baby have a real chance at success and happiness, my financial problems would be over." She returned to shredding the napkin. "I bought into it."

A plate crashed to the floor in the front of the café. All four of them jumped, then nervously laughed.

"Anyway, I agreed to give my baby up for adoption. Charlotte drew up papers, and I began to get money. My rent was paid. My electricity. I was able to get cable. And a phone." Her round eyes grew big. "The pantry always had food. It was good." She balled all the shredded pieces of napkin together. "Charlotte found adoptive parents who were very generous. Although I never met them in person, they sent me gift cards through Charlotte. And I knew the big payoff would come when I turned the baby over to her new parents."

Emily's stomach hurt, and she couldn't even think straight. That kind of sounded like she sold Olivia. It seemed wrong.

"I went into labor, and as soon as I saw her, I didn't want to go through with it. I snuck out of the hospital and went to see my parents. They let me in, and my mom seemed upset. I handed her the baby, and she cried and rocked her. She told me she'd been diagnosed with breast cancer, but she had no insurance to pay for treatment."

Although she had no intention of ever feeling sorry for Mackenzie Barnes, Emily found her heart softening toward the woman.

Inetta leaned over and put her hand on Mackenzie's. "So you knew then you had to go through with the adoption?"

Mackenzie nodded. "I couldn't lose my mother. The money

would pay for treatment. I took my baby and left. Charlotte had her goons out looking for me, and I handed the baby over without an argument." She wiped her eyes. "The money saved my mom, though. That's what I cling to now. And I'm not sure I would have been a good mother. I know my baby went to a family that wanted her desperately and loved her so much immediately. What I did was wrong—exchanging her for money—but I didn't know what else to do."

Emily glanced at Olivia and saw tears glistening in her eyes. Olivia had always wanted to be close to her grandparents. They lived in California. What if these grandparents would actually have spent time with her?

"You know I have to tell the sheriff, right?" Inetta eyed Mackenzie. "What Charlotte is doing is illegal."

Mackenzie nodded. "Yeah. I know. And what I did was wrong."

Inetta closed her notebook. "I have to get these young ladies home, but I'd really like you to come with me to talk to the sheriff."

Again, Mackenzie nodded. Then she stared at Emily and Olivia. "Which one of you i-is my daughter?"

Olivia squeezed Emily's hand really, really hard. "Me."

"I'm so, so sorry." Mackenzie pressed her lips together. "Have you had a happy life? Good parents who love you?"

Nodding, Olivia smiled. "Yeah."

TWENTY-THREE

Emily walked home from school with Olivia. "Inetta said the sheriff immediately got on the phone with the Marquette police to pick up Charlotte Tarver for questioning."

The wind whistled around them. The forecast called for snow for the next couple of days, possibly even a blizzard. Emily snuggled into her coat and thought of Naomi. They still had nothing on the case. *God, please protect Naomi. Let us find her. Please.*

"I wish Inetta could've called this morning with an update, but she probably doesn't know anything yet." *But man, oh man, were things happening. Poor Liv, to have to find out like this.* Emily hugged her. "I'm sorry, Liv."

"Me too." Olivia started down the street again

What did that mean for Mr. and Mrs. Webster? Emily stopped suddenly.

Olivia gave her a sad smile. "I can see you just thought of the same questions I've been wondering all day. How are my parents going to react? What about Mackenzie's family?" She shook her head. Tears slipped down her cheeks. "I wish we'd never started looking into my adoption." She stomped her foot. "I wish we'd never found that stupid picture. It's opened up a whole new set of problems. I mean, I love my parents, and I've always been happy. They love me, and they obviously wanted me. I'm not sure I want to get to know that other family at all. Especially not if it hurts my parents."

Emily couldn't think of a thing to say that would comfort Olivia, so she just squeezed her hand tightly. "Are you going to tell your parents, or let the sheriff?"

"I've thought about that all night and today, and I decided I'm going to tell them. They'll be less hurt if they hear from me why I went looking."

"I'm sorry, Liv. I shouldn't have pushed you to search."

"It's okay. I needed to know." But Olivia's face was still pale.

"How are you feeling? About—you know. The selling thing."

Olivia swallowed. "I guess I can understand it with the trouble she was in. I felt sorry for her when she was telling us. And I don't think my parents knew that was what was happening. I'm sure they were just grateful and wanted to help Mackenzie any way they could. I can't imagine them knowing that they were buying me."

Emily exhaled. At least Olivia wasn't freaked out about that part. "I agree. That doesn't sound like your parents at all." They reached Cottage Avenue, Emily's street. "Call me after you tell them."

"If I can."

Emily grabbed another hug, then raced toward home. Other than Charley and Sherlock greeting her with wagging tails, the house was silent as she entered, then she remembered Grandma had to take Timmy in for his checkup this afternoon. It felt really strange for ordinary things like doctor appointments to go on without Naomi. Timmy had been so little when Marika had left them that he'd forgotten her until she'd shown back up. What if Matthew forgot about Naomi? *God, please, please, pretty please... please bring Naomi home to us.*

She felt like her entire life was caught in some wicked tailspin.

Emily let Sherlock and Charley into the backyard, then headed to her room and grabbed her cell. She saw the voice mail indicator, but she had a call to make first. As she'd promised this morning, she quickly dialed Dad's number at the hardware store. He answered on the first ring. "Hi, Dad. Home safe and sound."

"Hi, sweetheart. I'll be leaving here in a few hours. Your grandma's picking up pizza on her way home."

Things had almost gotten to a new normal. Even Dad was back at work and letting Grandma oversee things at home. Emily wanted to scream for Naomi, but that wouldn't bring her back. "Okay. I'm going to do my homework. See you soon." She only had one algebra sheet to complete, which wouldn't take her long.

She checked her voice mail. It was Inetta, and she said it was urgent that Emily call her back immediately. Heart pounding, Emily called Inetta's cell phone.

"Emily, where are you?"

"In my room. What's going on?"

"Listen, my friend was able to trace the track-back program." Inetta spoke so fast her words almost tripped on each other.

"And?"

"The program originated from Charlotte Tarver's office. You must've triggered it when you did that initial search."

Emily could hear her pulse pounding.

"I had to take it to the sheriff. He's pretty upset you didn't tell him, by the way, and will probably tell your dad."

Great. Just when it felt like Dad had forgotten he'd grounded her, she'd be back in trouble.

"Are you there, Emily?"

"Yeah. I'm here."

"Listen, when the police went to pick up Charlotte Tarver for questioning last night, she wasn't there. They've cased out her home and her office, and there's no sign of her."

Emily lay back on her bed. "What does that mean?"

"Means that she's unaccounted for and we can assume she's dangerous. And we already know she's aware you and I both are involved in researching her." Inetta's voice was edged with concern. "Is your dad home yet?"

Emily sat up, grabbing her *Phantom of the Opera* pillow to her chest. "No, he's still at the store. Grandma's picking up pizza on her way home. Why?"

"Are you at home alone?" No mistaking the worry in Inetta's voice.

"Yes." Now she was getting creeped out. "Am I not safe?" All her mind could focus on was what Mackenzie had said about Charlotte's scary goons who had come after her when she snuck out of the hospital. Her mouth went dry.

"Just make sure the doors are locked until your dad gets home, okay? They're locked, right?"

She couldn't remember if she locked the front door behind her! She'd been thinking about Liv maybe having to leave, and Naomi missing, and the dogs . . .

"Emily! Go check. Right now. While I'm on the phone with you."

Now she was really scared. "Okay."

What if someone who worked for Charlotte was in the foyer,

waiting to attack her? Her heart pounded so hard she was sure it'd break her ribs. She managed to make it to the front door.

She let out a relieved breath. "The front door is locked."

"And the back?"

"The dogs are in the backyard." And she knew she hadn't locked that door. Emily raced to the kitchen door.

"Right. Good. Let the dogs in."

"Okay." She opened the door, and Charley and Sherlock rushed inside. She locked the door and dead bolted it, then grabbed a soda from the fridge. "Done."

"There's probably no issue at all, and I don't mean to scare you, but I just want you to take precautions. Sheriff Kaleva is in communication with the Marquette police, and they'll let him know as soon as they locate Charlotte."

She opened the soda and sat at the kitchen table. "Hey, Inetta, are you at the sheriff's now?" She picked at the pop-top before she took a sip.

"Yes, why?"

"Any update on Marika?"

Silence never sounded so loud. "Inetta?"

"Your dad hasn't told you?"

The tightening in her stomach returned. "Told me what?"

"I'm sorry, Emily. I just don't feel comfortable telling you. It's not my place to say anything."

Emily curled her hand into a fist. "I deserve to know."

"And your dad will probably tell you."

"I just got off the phone with him, and he didn't say anything about Marika."

"He's probably waiting to tell you in person."

"Come on, Inetta." Emily groaned. "Please. I won't let anyone know you told me first, I promise."

Silence.

"Inetta?"

A loud sigh. "I shouldn't, but you're right, you do deserve to know."

Emily sat up straighter as Charley and Sherlock plopped down on their favorite rug in the kitchen. "Thank you."

"Marika was charged with arson and is in jail."

The news didn't even faze Emily. Not anymore. Not after everything Marika had done. "Did she ever explain why she poisoned Charley?"

The dog looked up at his name. Emily smiled and took a sip of her soda.

"I didn't actually hear, but one of the deputies told me she'd claimed to have only wanted Charley disabled enough that she could get a chance to talk to you alone."

"Why?" Marika had spoken to her in the woods at the homecoming celebration, but nothing so important as to poison Charley. "What did she want to talk to me about?"

"Apparently she thought you could tell your dad you wanted to spend some time with her and he'd agree." Inetta snorted. "Of course Sheriff Kaleva did a little digging and found out about the inheritance, which is what she wanted most. I'm sorry, but I think that's the whole reason she came back to Rock Harbor. Just to try and wheedle it from you."

"What inheritance?"

"Your dad didn't tell you about that either?"

"Inetta!"

She sighed. "Emily, you're so going to get me in trouble."

Emily's stomach churned. "What inheritance?"

"Marika's aunt died. She never had any children and had originally left her estate to Marika. Once Marika had you, the aunt changed the will to leave her estate to you. Soon after finding that out, Marika stopped seeing her aunt, never even telling her when she had Timmy."

Emily shook her head. She didn't understand any of this.

"The aunt died a few weeks ago, and the executor is concluding the estate. He had to contact Marika to locate you. She refused to tell him where you were, but he found out anyway and contacted your father." Inetta's voice softened. "I'm sorry, Em. She's just here for the money."

"That's no surprise."

But her lips felt numb. Her mother really didn't care about her at all. She hadn't changed, and she wasn't sorry. But Emily found it still didn't change the fact that she had forgiven her. It didn't feel good, but she wasn't angry or bitter anymore. Bree was right. Forgiving Marika made her feel better, even if it never changed Marika a bit.

Woof! Charley and Sherlock raced to the door, tails wagging.

"Hey, I've got to go. I think Grandma and the boys are home. I'll need to help her."

"Okay. I'll talk to you later."

"Thanks, Inetta. For telling me."

"Yeah, just try not to get me in trouble."

Emily disconnected the call and headed into the living room, where Timmy nearly ran her over as he ran inside with two large pizza boxes. "Hey, Dad's home too, so we can eat."

Matthew followed, then Grandma. "Hello, dear. How was your day?" She planted a kiss on Emily's cheek before putting her purse on the table in the entryway.

"Good."

Dad brought up the rear, closing the door behind him. He wore a scowl. "I'd like to talk to you, young lady."

"I'll get the boys their dinner." Grandma headed into the kitchen.

Dad sat on the couch and pointed at the chair across from him. Emily slunk into the seat. "Yes, sir?"

"I had a call from Mason. Regarding your computer."

"Dad, I'm sorry. I wanted to tell you, I did, but I couldn't without telling you . . . about something else."

"About Olivia being adopted?"

Her heart sank to her toes. "You knew?"

He shook his head. "I only found out when Mason called. Apparently Inetta Harris told Mason quite the story, along with a Mackenzie Barnes."

She ran her teeth over her bottom lip. "Dad, I'm really sorry. I'd promised Olivia I wouldn't say anything to anyone. You understand how that is, right? You've told me we have to honor our promises." *Please, God, let him remember his lecture to me about not breaking our word.*

Dad looked like he'd eaten a sour apple.

"I'm really, really sorry."

"Okay. I can understand you not wanting to break a promise."

Yes!

"However, you need to be careful about making promises like that in the future. Sometimes big secrets can put people in danger."

"Like how the secret of my inheritance put Charley in danger?"

Dad's face went white, then very, very red.

Uh-oh. She really should've stopped that from slipping out.

TWENTY-FOUR

"So, basically, I have a college fund totally set up." Emily lodged her cell between her cheek and shoulder and tossed the throw toy to Sherlock, who raced across the bedroom to grab the squeaky duck.

"That's awesome," Olivia replied.

"Yeah, but I'm still upset Dad didn't tell me right away. He said he and Naomi talked it over and decided they didn't want to tell me because they were afraid I wouldn't study as hard if I knew I had college paid for." Did they think she wouldn't do her best anyway?

"At least you know the money's there for college no matter what though."

Emily nodded as she stared at her ceiling. "Yeah, there's that. At least he didn't ground me again for not telling him everything we've been up to, even though he was really mad."

"I'd take a grounding over the crying here. My mom hasn't stopped bawling since we talked."

Man, oh man. She really shouldn't be complaining at all right now about such a secret. It was nothing compared to Olivia's family secrets. "I can't believe they sent you to your room while they called the sheriff and talked to him."

"I know, right? Like I can't be part of whatever conversation they're having? Sheesh, it's about *me*. I'm the one who should be in the middle of the conversation. I'm the innocent party here."

Emily detected the hurt in her best friend's voice, the pain she desperately tried to hide. "I'm so sorry, Liv."

"It's done, right? Not like we can turn back time and have me *not* sold." Olivia sniffed.

Emily felt smaller than small. Here she was, complaining about having a college fund set up that she didn't know about, and her best friend was in agony. *God, please comfort Liv. She's so upset right now. Please love on her a lot.*

Olivia continued, "Anyway, once they find Charlotte Tarver and figure out how many babies she basically sold, the sheriff feels likes Mackenzie's testimony will really help bring Charlotte to justice."

Timmy burst into her room. *Without* knocking.

"Emily, Dad wants you. Right now. He looks mad. You're probably in trouble again." He stuck his tongue out at her, then ran into the hall where Charley waited.

She gritted her teeth. "I've got to go. Dad wants me for something." She shoved off the bed. "It's gonna be okay, Liv. I know it. For both of us." She prayed she was right.

"You wanted me?" she asked Dad as she plopped onto the couch beside Grandma. Timmy, the little snake, wasn't anywhere in the room.

"I just got a call from Mason."

Every muscle went tense at Dad's tone. "And?" Her heart rate went into overdrive.

"The Marquette police have reason to believe Charlotte Tarver is in Rock Harbor."

"Has Sheriff Kaleva found her?"

Dad shook his head. "He's looking. He's got all the deputies looking, and the state police too."

Emily wanted so badly to find this woman who'd caused Olivia such pain.

"Don't worry. Mason's doing everything he can. He'll find her."

"You know all about the investigator she had, right? The one looking into Inetta?"

"Yes, Mason filled me in on all the details." Dad's brow scrunched. "That's why I get upset with you, Emily. Because you put yourself in danger without even thinking about it." He leaned forward, resting his elbows on his knees. "I love you so much . . . when you do dangerous things, it scares me."

"Oh, Daddy." She moved into his lap and curled into his hug, just like she'd done when she was little bitty. "I love you too."

"You're going to wear a hole in my rug if you don't stop," Grandma said. "It's a real Persian, you know."

Emily stopped pacing but tapped her foot against the beautiful rug in Grandma's Blue Bonnet Bed and Breakfast. "I can't help it. Dad's taking forever. I want to know everything they found out about Charlotte Tarver."

Sheriff Kaleva had called about an hour ago, telling them the state troopers had picked up the attorney on the highway. She'd been brought to Rock Harbor's sheriff office and was being questioned. Dad had gone to the station with Mr. Webster for moral support.

He'd called ten minutes ago and said he was on his way home. He'd sounded . . . odd. It didn't take ten minutes to drive a little over two blocks. Well, the weather had gotten a bit rough. Strong wind and snow flurries already swirling high in the sky. Forecast for an early winter storm was predicted.

"Patience has never been your strong suit, has it, dear?" Grandma chuckled. "Why don't you help me put stamps on these invitations?"

Emily stared at the envelopes with addresses written in beautiful calligraphy. "Maybe we should cancel the party, considering everything."

"Even though there's controversy regarding Olivia's adoption, Mr. and Mrs. Webster are no less married. This party is for their anniversary. Of course it shouldn't be canceled."

Maybe she was right. Emily took a seat and grabbed a book of stamps.

"I think a party is just what Olivia's family needs. They're all hurting so much, each in their own way." Grandma made tsking noises.

Emily hung her head. This was all her fault. She was the one who'd pushed Olivia to get to the truth.

Grandma shook her head, but not before Emily noticed the tears in her eyes. "Naomi's been missing for a week today, and I feel like my heart's been ripped right from my chest. We have to find her."

The sound of gravel crunching in the drive pushed Emily to her feet. The book of stamps shot to the floor.

Grandma waved her away. "I'll get them. You go see your dad before you have a breakdown."

Emily rushed to the front entrance, where Dad was stepping over the threshold.

His face had more color and liveliness than she'd seen on him in a long time. "News?"

"Let's go into the parlor with your grandma." His steps were sure and quick.

This had to be good news.

Grandma looked up as they entered. Emily trailed and sat on the love seat.

"I talked with Mason. He's completed his interview with Charlotte Tarver and is filing charges against her."

"What did she say?" Emily couldn't wait for Dad to draw the story out. This was her best friend's life.

Dad held up his hand. "Once Mason told her he knew about Mackenzie and Olivia, she realized she was facing charges and not just disbarment. Knowing the charges would stick, she confessed to having Naomi kidnapped."

Grandma gasped. Emily felt every muscle in her body go limp. Charlotte had kidnapped Naomi?

Dad rocked back on his heels. "She said when the track-back program was activated by your system, she got Naomi's information."

Emily's stomach twisted like a pretzel. She'd been right—her research is what had gotten Naomi taken after all.

Dad continued, "Charlotte hired someone to determine why Naomi was digging into Charlotte and the adoptions. The night of the fire, he took a picture of Naomi with the Websters. When Charlotte saw it, she recognized them, and with Olivia in the picture, she remembered the situation. Scared that her baby-selling ring was about to be revealed, she ordered her associate to kidnap Naomi."

"What could she hope to gain? Surely she knew Naomi would eventually talk?" Grandma's voice wobbled.

"According to her confession, she planned to keep Naomi hidden away just long enough for her to leave the country without suspicion. She carried on business as usual for the week, clearing up cases and such and letting everyone know in the office she had a very sick relative she needed to leave town to go check on."

Emily's grip tightened on Grandma's shoulders. "So, where's Naomi now?"

Dad's eyes darkened. "That's what she wouldn't say. Not until she gets some sort of deal from the district attorney."

"We still don't know where my daughter is?" Grandma's voice was filled with emotion.

"Not right now, but Mason's on the phone with the state's attorney, trying to get them to do anything for Charlotte to give up Naomi's location." Dad's tone went deep. "Mason ordered me to leave. He said because of the storm forecast, but I think it's because he didn't want me near Charlotte Tarver."

"So what are we supposed to do?" Grandma asked.

"We have to trust Mason will do everything to get Naomi's location." Dad stared out the front window. "Until Mason calls, we just wait."

He faced them. "And pray."

TWENTY-FIVE

The clouds hung low and threatening in the frigid air when Emily stepped onto the back deck to call Sherlock. She whistled, but there was no answering happy bark. Cupping her hands to her mouth, she shouted for him. Silly puppy was probably wrestling with a leaf or something. She frowned. Was that a break in the fence? She hurried down the steps and examined the hole. A tuft of fur was stuck in it. Sherlock must have escaped through here.

She had to find her puppy. The woods weren't safe for a pup his size, especially with the blizzard rolling in. She stepped back inside and went to find her dad. Wearing a strange look on his face, Dad had his cell phone to his ear and was listening intently. Her pulse jumped in her throat, and she went to stand near him. He pulled her closer so she could listen in on the conversation.

Sheriff Kaleva's voice held excitement. "So we have somewhere to search. Charlotte told us her accomplice put Naomi ashore and was going to release her, but Naomi ran off into the woods."

"Where?" Dad asked, his voice tight.

"On the northern edge of the Porkies, she said."

"Not that far from here," Dad said. "Did you call Bree?"

"She's on her way with Samson. We need Charley too. He has the most connection with Naomi," the sheriff said.

"I'll bring him. He can go with Bree."

Here was her chance! Emily grabbed his arm. "Dad, I want to go!"

He shook his head and moved the phone away from Emily. "Sorry, Mason, Emily is begging to go, but I don't want her out with the blizzard coming. Bree is the best. She'll find Naomi."

Dad finished his conversation. "I heard we'd be dealing with weather. We'll find her. See you in a few minutes." He ended the call.

Emily blinked back tears. "I want to help find her, Dad."

He shrugged on his coat. "I know you do, but I can't risk your health. Your grandma would have my hide if I let you go out in that storm. We're supposed to get nearly two feet of snow and high winds."

She bit her lip and swallowed hard. "I have to go find Sherlock. He got out through the fence."

He glanced at his watch. "Okay, but be back here in an hour whether you find him or not. Understand?"

She nodded reluctantly. "I'm sure he hasn't gone far. Why can't I search with Bree for at least a little while?"

"Someone would have to bring you back, and we can't leave the search if the dogs find her trail. I'm taking the snowmobile." His face was set with determination. "I'm not coming back without her."

He grabbed Charley's leash from the hook by the door. "I'll let your grandma know what's happening."

Still unhappy, Emily pulled on her coat and gloves. She yanked her hood up and stepped out the back door. "Sherlock!" No answering bark came on the stiffening breeze.

She opened the gate and stepped through to the path leading into the woods. His doggy paw prints in the dusting of snow led her on. He'd gone this way for sure. Probably chasing squirrels.

Or trying to find his daddy, Samson.

Tucking her hands in her pockets, she followed the prints. The wind grew fiercer and the temperature began to drop. Walking kept her warm though.

"Sherlock!" The wind snatched her cry away. What if an eagle had grabbed him? Or a mountain lion?

At the thought, she looked around uneasily. While no panther had been spotted this close to town, it wasn't impossible. Who knew what lurked in the shadows and trees? She shouted for the puppy again. Glancing at her *Phantom of the Opera* watch, she realized she had already been gone for a half hour. She should start back if she was going to obey her dad. But she couldn't leave Sherlock out here. The blizzard might kill him. He'd be lost and not know which way to go. She'd just stay another fifteen minutes.

Quickening her steps, she rushed along the trail, pausing occasionally to yell for the dog. She had to find him! Through the trees, she could see the black clouds. The storm was supposed to hit around one. Her dad would kill her if she didn't turn around and head for home. Maybe she could call him. She felt in her pocket for her cell phone, but she couldn't find it. Had she dropped it? She was going to be in big trouble if she'd lost it.

Sighing, she turned around. Then she heard a distant bark and whirled. "Sherlock?" She ran toward the sound. "Here, boy, come to me."

The bark came again, but it sounded like he was staying

in one place. Could he be trapped? She put on an extra burst of speed and hurdled over a low-lying bush. Big flakes of snow wafted to the ground, and she glanced at her watch again.

Oh no! She'd forgotten to change the time. Daylight saving time had ended last night. It was going on one. No wonder Dad had very specifically told her to be back in an hour. The flakes fell faster as she hollered for her puppy again. His bark was frenzied, just past a big pine tree.

He was jumping up and down but still not running to meet her. Then she saw the form stretched out in the snow.

Naomi!

Emily ran until she stood over her stepmom. Naomi's eyes were closed in her pale face. Sherlock huddled close as if to keep her warm. Tears started in Emily's eyes. "Naomi!" She knelt beside her and touched her cheek. "Please don't be dead."

Naomi's cheek was cold but pliable. Her eyelids fluttered, and there was a faint movement up and down of her chest. "Thank you, God." Emily's voice broke. She couldn't have withstood losing Naomi.

If only she'd brought a thermos of coffee or hot chocolate. Emily slipped her arm under Naomi's head. "Naomi, can you hear me?"

Naomi licked her lips, and her eyes opened. Her gaze was unfocused, then sharpened when she looked at Emily. She groaned and struggled to get up. "Emily? Am I dreaming? I thought I heard Sherlock."

Emily cradled her close. "You did. He found you and refused to leave you even when I called him."

Naomi smiled faintly. "Good dog. Where are we?"

"Nearly an hour from home. And there's a blizzard blowing in any minute."

"Help me sit up." Naomi winced as Emily lifted her. "I think I broke my leg."

That changed everything. "I've got to find us some shelter then. We won't make it home before it hits." Emily glanced around the woods. She knew this area well. "There's an old miner's cabin that way." She gestured to the north. "It's farther from the house, but we can make it there before the storm hits, I think."

"I'm not sure I can walk. Can you see if you can find me a branch to use as a crutch?"

"I'll see what I can do. Stay, Sherlock." Like the puppy would do anything else. He was so happy to see Naomi, he wasn't going anywhere.

Emily quickly began to pick through the underbrush for a branch. She found a fairly sturdy one with a forked end and took it to Naomi. "Will this work?"

"I think so. I'm going to need help getting to my feet."

Emily let Naomi lean on her and managed to get her upright with the branch under her arm. "This way."

They moved slowly through the snow that was beginning to fall faster. "I see it!" Emily urged Naomi as fast as she dared. The snow and wind picked up until it was hard to see the dark outline of the structure ahead. "Nearly there."

Five more feet and they stood in front of the door. Emily pushed on it. "I think it's locked. Let me see if I can get in the window." She went around to the back and found a window she could shove open. It was barely large enough to squeeze through, but she finally fell inside the cabin. The cessation of wind was a blessed relief. She scrambled to her feet and rushed to the door, where she threw the dead bolt.

Naomi was leaning against the cabin with her eyes closed. She was even paler. Emily took her arm. "We're here, Naomi. There's a cot here. Let's get your leg up." She helped Naomi inside. Sherlock ran past their feet, and Emily shut the door behind them.

Now they just had to wait out the storm and pray for the searchers to find them.

God, are you there? Thank you for keeping Naomi safe and letting me find her. Emily smiled as Sherlock sniffed around the door to the cabin. *Well, thanks for letting Sherlock find her. But, God, it's really, really cold in here, and Naomi's hurt. She's not really doing so great. I know Dad and Bree are out looking and searching. If you could, please, God, would you let them find us sooner rather than later?*

Naomi moaned in her sleep, her face registering the pain as her leg moved.

Emily felt her head. Hot again. The fever was back, and there wasn't a thing Emily could do. She'd brought in snowballs and fed Naomi snow, but her fever still raged like the wind blasted outside.

According to her watch, they'd been in the cabin for only an hour, but already snow was stacking up outside. Another hour or two and they'd be snowed in.

What am I supposed to do?

Sherlock whined at the door. Poor thing, he probably had to go to the bathroom. Emily eased open the door, and he shot out through the crack. She shut the door back and looked at her watch. In five minutes, she'd call him back if he hadn't come back already.

"Emily!" Naomi's voice was so weak.

She rushed to her stepmom's side. "I'm here, Naomi."

Naomi touched her face. "I thought I'd dreamed you found me."

"No, I'm right here. We're safe in this cabin until Dad and Bree find us."

"Good. I thought he'd come back."

"Who? Charlotte's partner?"

"You know her?" Naomi's voice was a whisper.

Emily nodded. "Sheriff Kaleva has her in custody. She told him an accomplice brought you back to shore to release you, but you escaped."

"Evil woman." Naomi swallowed loudly. "And the guy is just plain mean. He didn't feed me much."

Emily ran a hand to smooth Naomi's matted and greasy hair. "What did they do to you?" she whispered.

"Only gave me water and vitamins." Naomi coughed, then grimaced as if the movement hurt her more than her leg. "To keep me weak so I couldn't fight back."

She kissed Naomi's forehead. "I'm so sorry, Naomi. It's all my fault. If I wouldn't have searched for Olivia's birth mother, the track-back program wouldn't have been activated and she wouldn't have sent him to follow you. He took a picture of you and Mrs. Webster and Olivia, and that's what made her hire him to kidnap you. I'm so sorry." Tears choked her and she finally took a breath.

Naomi smiled weakly, but a smile. "I have no idea what you're talking about." She swallowed again. "But it's not your fault. And you've saved me. You and Sherlock."

Sherlock!

Emily rushed to the door and flung it open.

Wind pushed a sheet of snow right into her, stinging her face. "Sherlock!" She cupped her hands around her mouth and yelled again, "Sherlock! Here, boy."

A gust of air nearly knocked her over. She glanced over her shoulder to see Naomi shivering on the cot. Emily took a step out of the door and pulled it closed behind her. "Sherlock!"

In the distance, she could barely make out barking.

"Sherlock! Here, boy. Sherlock!"

Woof! Woof!

Emily's heart leaped. That wasn't her puppy's bark. That was—

Samson and Charley burst through the tree line, Sherlock on their heels. All three barked and jumped up on Emily, knocking her to the ground.

And then she was in Dad's arms. "I was so worried about you when your grandma called and said you weren't home. Then the storm hit and Sherlock found us. He led us right to you." He squeezed her tight. "I told you I loved you too much and didn't want you doing dangerous things like this."

She smiled. "Dad, Bree . . . we found Naomi. Sherlock did."

"What?" Dad's arms around her tightened.

"Where?" Bree reached for the doorknob even as she asked.

Dad rushed to Naomi and swept her into his arms. "Naomi!"

Emily's stepmom opened her eyes, stared into Dad's face, and smiled. "Donovan, what took you so long?"

Emily didn't even look away from the gushy stuff going on. Her eyes welled with tears, and she ran to join them in a group hug.

EPILOGUE

The anniversary party was a smashing success. The bed-and-breakfast was decorated with photos and mementos from Mr. and Mrs. Webster's twenty-five years together. The cake Naomi had ordered with the design of their wedding picture was beautiful. Even the weather had cooperated with a sunny sky and temperatures up in the forties.

Olivia walked over to Emily and threw an arm around her shoulder. "Everything's just perfect."

Emily watched her dad hand a cup of punch to Naomi, whose leg cast had been decorated with sparkles for the occasion. Dr. Parker said the X-rays showed it'd been broken in two places as she'd tried to escape, but that it would heal fine and she'd be back search-and-rescuing before they knew it.

Naomi didn't talk much about her week in captivity, saying she didn't want to give Charlotte Tarver any more time in their lives. But she'd gone through a bad week, Emily could tell.

Timmy and Matthew had been reluctant to leave her side

since her return. And Charley? Well, the golden retriever almost didn't let her out of his sight. But Emily thought that all of that was probably good. Naomi needed her family around her while she healed.

Emily grinned at her best friend. "Yeah, I'd have to agree: life's pretty perfect right now."

"Olivia," Mrs. Webster called.

Both girls turned. Olivia went still as a board as her mother and Mackenzie approached. Emily silently took Olivia's hand.

"Olivia," Mrs. Webster said. "You've already met your biological mother, Mackenzie."

Liv squeezed Emily's hand. "Hello."

Tears fell down Mackenzie's face. "You are so beautiful." She looked at Mrs. Webster. "You've been a wonderful mother. Thank you." She looked back at Olivia. "I hope there's room in your life for me too. Now that we've found each other, I'd really like to get to know you. If that's okay with you and your parents. I know the way I went about it was all wrong, but I'm really glad you were adopted. I've always missed you and thought about you, but I was really young, and I think you've had a much better life with your parents than you would have had with me. "

Olivia let go of Emily's hand and hugged Mackenzie, who hugged her back, but also reached to Mrs. Webster and pulled her in against them. "I'd like to get to know you too." Olivia's voice was choked.

Emily pressed her lips together. She wouldn't cry. Instead she turned and moved away.

Sherlock rushed by, barking as he chased Samson in the bed-and-breakfast's backyard.

Thank you, God. For everything. She smiled and headed to her family.

Life was, indeed, pretty perfect for the moment. And that was just the way she liked it.

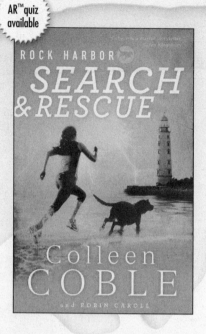

FROM AWARD-WINNING AUTHOR COLLEEN COBLE COMES HER FIRST SERIES FOR YOUNG ADVENTURERS: A MIXTURE OF MYSTERY, SUSPENSE, ACTION—AND ADORABLE PUPPIES!

Eighth-grader Emily O'Reilly is obsessed with all things Search-and-Rescue. The almost-fourteen-year-old spends every spare moment on rescues with her stepmom Naomi and her canine partner Charley. But when an expensive necklace from a renowned jewelry artist is stolen under her care at the fall festival, Emily is determined to prove her innocence to a town that has immediately labeled her guilty.

As Emily sets out to restore her reputation, she isn't prepared for the surprises she and the Search-and-Rescue dogs uncover along the way. Will Emily ever find the real thief?

BY COLLEEN COBLE

www.tommynelson.com

www.colleencoble.com

IF YOU WERE DESCENDED FROM ANGELS, HOW WOULD YOU USE YOUR POWERS?

Check out the exciting new *Son of Angels* series!

Jonah, Eliza, and Jeremiah Stone are one-quarter angel, which seems totally cool until it lands them in the middle of a war between angels and fallen angels. As they face the Fallen, they will find their faith tested like never before . . .

By Jerel Law

www.tommynelson.com

www.jerellaw.com

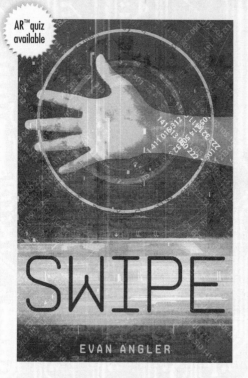